**"I agreed to marry you,"** Josselyn panted out at Cenzo, her lips faintly swollen and her brown eyes wild.

"Not to take part in whatever sick revenge fantasy this is," she continued. "I refuse to be a pawn in your game."

"You can be any piece on the board that you like," he replied, trying to gather himself. "But it will still be my board, Josselyn."

And he watched something wash over her, intense and deep, and realized that he was holding on to her as if he wished to keep her with him.

He let her go, lifting up his hands theatrically. "By all means. Run and hide if that makes you feel more powerful."

He kept his hands in the air, his mock surrender, and laughed at her as he stepped back.

Because he'd forgotten, entirely, that they stood on those narrow stairs.

She had kissed him silly.

It was his own mocking laughter that stayed with him as he fell, a seeming slow-motion slide backward. He saw h̶̶̶̶̶ from beneath him.

Nothing but her lov

And then—*nothing*.

*USA TODAY* bestselling, RITA® Award—nominated and critically acclaimed author **Caitlin Crews** has written more than one hundred books and counting. She has a master's and PhD in English literature, thinks everyone should read more category romance and is always available to discuss her beloved alpha heroes. Just ask. She lives in the Pacific Northwest with her comic book artist husband, is always planning her next trip and will never, ever, read all the books in her to-be-read pile. Thank goodness.

# Caitlin Crews

## THE SICILIAN'S FORGOTTEN WIFE

Recycling programs for this product may not exist in your area.

ISBN-13: 978-1-335-56797-0

The Sicilian's Forgotten Wife

Copyright © 2021 by Caitlin Crews

This edition published by arrangement with Harlequin Books S.A.

For questions and comments about the quality of this book, please contact us at CustomerService@Harlequin.com.

Harlequin Enterprises ULC
22 Adelaide St. West, 40th Floor
Toronto, Ontario M5H 4E3, Canada
www.Harlequin.com

Printed in U.S.A.

# THE SICILIAN'S
# FORGOTTEN WIFE

# CHAPTER ONE

JOSSELYN CHRISTIE DID not expect to enjoy her wedding day.

It wasn't that kind of wedding. She wasn't that kind of bride—the sort who had dreamed her whole life of a white dress, a battalion of attendants, and a ceremony filled with personal details and love—which was just as well, because there was an appropriate dress, but no battalion. And the ceremony had been about the solemnity of marriage itself, not the couple getting married. A necessity as the couple hardly knew each other.

Josselyn understood it wouldn't be a modern marriage, either, bristling with romance and mushy public declarations. Enjoyment really wasn't on the menu.

But she had hoped for some degree of civility from the groom.

Her reception was in full swing in the ballroom. Old money Philadelphia milled genteelly around the ballroom in all their usual glory, here in her father's house on the historic Christie estate, considered one of the most elegant addresses in Pennsylvania. And therefore, by definition, in the whole of America.

*Just ask anyone here*, Josselyn thought, as close to amused as she'd been in months.

The money on display in this ballroom tonight was so ancient that those who had inherited it didn't call themselves Old Philadelphians. They preferred *proper* Philadelphians, or *perennial* Philadelphians, depending on the audience. But one thing they could all agree upon was that they were the direct—and in some cases, indirect—descendants of the first families of Ye Olde Pennsylvania colony. They felt, almost universally, that their bloodlines made them personally responsible for settling the state of Pennsylvania—and by inference, therefore, these United States.

If she listened closely, Josselyn was sure she could hear some of the snootier guests murmuring the so-called Philadelphia Rosary just under the sound of the band, that old rhyme of worthy Pennsylvania family names.

*Morris, Norris, Rush and Chew...*

*Drinker, Dallas, Coxe and Pugh...*

The Christies had Whartons on one side and Pennypackers on the other. Their money was old, their blood blue, and Josselyn supposed she should always have known that she was destined for a future precisely like the one she was embarking upon tonight. She should not have imagined that, somehow, she would be saved from sacrificing herself to her family name like all the blue-blooded brides before her.

"You look pensive, my dear," came a familiar voice from beside her, startling Josselyn out of her gloomy thoughts. Thoughts of bloodlines and sacrifice did not inspire the average bride to beam about her reception, apparently. But she smiled almost instantly anyway, the usual rush of affection taking her over.

Even today.

Especially today.

Because she loved her father to distraction. She would do anything for him, as this day proved. She smiled down at him now, remembering when he had seemed bigger and stronger than anything that might threaten her. Now the years had seemed to shrink the elderly Archibald Christie, but she could see the differences in him already. Now that he had settled his daughter's affairs as well as he could, in the best way he knew.

Because he believed that this marriage would keep Josselyn safe. And having lost her mother and brother, even if the accident was so long ago now, Josselyn had always understood that her safety was her father's primary concern.

Even at such a cost.

Her gaze moved of its own accord toward the towering, brooding figure across the ballroom, engaged in deep conversation with a collection of other billionaires—all hanging on his every word, naturally—but she forced her eyes back to her father. No good could possibly come of making herself more anxious. Worrying would not change what lay ahead of her.

"I think the beginning of any marriage requires some level of pensiveness," Josselyn said, but lightly. She slid her arm around her father's shoulders, trying not to notice that he felt more frail than he should have. Because noticing it only broke her heart anew. And her poor heart was in enough trouble today. "Some sober reflection, perhaps. Clearheadedness and calm in preparation for what is to come."

She could feel her father sigh a bit, next to her. They stood side by side, looking out over all the very best people who danced, drank, and cavorted beneath the gleaming lights. And who, Josselyn knew, would give not one thought to her again. Not one single thought.

Because this was the kind of wedding people attended for any number of reasons, but none of them having to do with celebrating love. And really, Josselyn had no one to blame but herself for imagining love would ever factor into her situation.

More fool her.

"I understand that this is not, perhaps, what you wanted," Archibald said in his usual tone, gruffness overlaid with seven decades of innate polish. "I may be an old fool, but I hope I'm not entirely delusional."

"Of course not, Papa," Josselyn murmured. Placating him, of course. She'd told herself a million times that she needed to stop doing it, because surely it was time she strode forth and claimed her own life. But no matter how many New Year's resolutions she made, she couldn't quite bring herself to stop.

That was what affection did. It made her act against her own interests, and she couldn't even say she'd minded too much until now.

Her father was many things, but easily placated was not among them. "You might think that I am a doddering idiot. I accept that. But I think, in time, you'll see that all of this is for the best."

"I understand," Josselyn said as calmly as she could. "If I didn't understand, I would never have agreed."

And that was the thing. She had agreed.

No matter how overwrought she might have felt when she'd walked down the aisle this afternoon, no one had forced her to do it. There had been no gun at her back, no threats, no direct pressure. Josselyn had taken her father's arm of her own free will and walked down that long aisle to her own doom.

Her father was drawn into conversation with an old family friend, but Josselyn stayed where she was. She smoothed her hands down the front of her exquisite gown, a near replica of the one her gorgeous mother had worn at her wedding. It had been Josselyn's great joy, if laced with the usual bitter sweetness, to hold on tight to that connection today. She ordered herself to breathe. To smile. Instead, against her will, her gaze was drawn back across the room to where *he* still stood, holding court in his typically unyielding fashion.

Cenzo Falcone, a man so widely feared and admired that his first name was usually enough to create commotion. *Cenzo*, they would whisper, then shudder, and no explanation was needed. Cenzo, descended through European royalty and considered Sicilian nobility, heir to crumbling castles across the globe and a fortune so vast it was said a man could not possibly spend it all in ten lifetimes.

Cenzo Falcone. Her husband.

God have mercy on her soul.

A passing waiter offered Josselyn a drink and she took it gratefully. She was tempted to neck it straight down, but she managed to control herself. Rendering herself insensate might be appealing—more than appealing, at the moment—but she doubted it would end well. Because the wedding and the reception were one thing, but the clock was ticking. And all too soon, Josselyn would have to leave this place.

With him.

As his wife.

She took a small sip of the sparkling wine and kept her gaze trained on the groom.

Her husband. Maybe if she kept calling him what he was, this whole thing would seem more real. Or less overwhelming. Because many people had husbands. They were thick on the ground. There was surely no need to find the term intimidating.

Maybe if she called him what he was, she would find her way to some kind of peace with her new role as his wife.

When she looked across the room at this man who had stood up before all these people—there at the head of the long aisle, unsmiling while tightly coiled power swirled all around him, his brutally sensual features a raw assault—her mouth went dry. When the wedding ceremony had been hours ago now.

It was something about those arresting eyes of his, copper and gold, as if he was making a mockery of all the robber barons who had made their fortunes here. Many of whose descendants were currently eating canapés and having a waltz across the ballroom floor.

*Breathe*, Josselyn ordered herself.

Their courtship, such as it was, had been conducted over the course of only two in-person meetings. The first meeting had occurred two years ago, in Northeast Harbor, Maine, where Josselyn's family had been summering for more than a hundred years. Josselyn had been acting as her father's social secretary since she'd graduated from Vassar four years before, and she had been spending the cool afternoon catching up on his correspondence in the blue and white sitting room where her mother had once sat and read to her.

And everything seemed divided into before and after that fateful meeting.

There was before, when she had been writing out notes by hand because her father prided himself on his old school, old world approach to things. *The secret to my success, my dear*, he would tell her jovially, when they both knew the real secret was having been born a Christie. And better still, the male heir.

Josselyn had been humming her favorite summer anthem beneath her breath, silly and bright. She had been thinking that the breeze coming in through the windows was lovely, but it was making her a bit cold, so she might run up in a moment to grab a light scarf. Her plans had involved a walk later. Possibly a sail, though her father didn't like it when she sailed out alone, so she rarely did it. It had been a Thursday, so her father's housekeeper was off and it would fall to Josselyn to prepare their supper later. She was planning on a cold soup with fresh vegetables from the garden.

Such a mundane, quiet summer's day in the middle of what she'd considered a happy little life. At least, Josselyn thought she'd been happy. It seemed to her she must have been, in those last, sweet moments before everything changed.

"Josselyn," her father had called from the parlor in the front part of the house. "Come meet our guest."

She could remember the suppressed excitement in her father's voice and had stood quickly, frowning, because she hadn't expected any visitors that day. Her father's interests ran mainly to his golf game and his club when he was in Maine, and when he threw the odd dinner party—rarely more than a handful all summer—he had Josselyn plan them well in advance.

Still, there were longtime family friends and what seemed like half of Philadelphia's upper crust all around on the rocky, craggy island, some twenty miles from Bar Harbor. Any one of them might have stopped by.

Josselyn had tried in vain to smooth down her usually long and straight dark hair, gone thick, wispy, and frizzy with the sea air. She'd been thinking a little bit crossly that she shouldn't need to worry about her appearance with no advance warning, but knew she would have worn something more appropriate if she'd known she'd have to appear in the parlor today. Appropriate by her father's definition, that was, whose take on modesty seemed to have gotten stuck midway through the previous century.

Then she'd walked into the room and promptly forgotten her Bermuda shorts and soft chambray shirt, clothes better suited for, say, a spell in the garden where there would be dirt. Her father was seated in his usual chair, and she noted distractedly that he was beaming. But that wasn't the alarming part.

The alarming part was Cenzo Falcone, leaning up against the gentle old fireplace across the bright and happy room.

Dark and brooding and the end of everything.

She couldn't remember what he'd chosen to wear, though she had the vague impression of a suitable shirt and dark trousers. But all she'd really registered was *him*. All that power. All that unrelenting intensity of those curious eyes of his, as if they were ancient coins his ancestors might have traded in, off in lost kingdoms long ago. The impression of his chiseled male beauty, almost alien in its severity. The close-cropped dark hair, the nose of a Roman emperor, the sense that whole nations rose and fell on his wide shoulders.

The man would have been an affront to the senses in a city of glass and concrete. Somehow, there on the coast of Maine, he was more like a terrible outrage. A dark and knowing storm that had rendered her powerless at a glance.

Her ears had been ringing, her heart had taken up a terrible pounding in her chest, and Josselyn had felt simultaneously winded and wild. She'd wanted to run out of the house that had always been her refuge, as fast as she could until she hit the water. The moody Atlantic, where she could take her chances with the currents that might sweep her off, all the way to Iceland and beyond, if she was lucky.

Though at that moment, Cenzo's eyes heavy upon her for the first time, drowning had seemed like a pleasant alternative. And also redundant.

Josselyn had stayed where she was, rooted to the spot, while her father mouthed some pleasantries, conducted whatever he considered appropriate introductions that she hardly heard, and then made everything worse by quitting the room.

Leaving Josselyn all alone with this man who had looked at her like she had chosen this fate. And made it clear he did not think highly of her for the choice.

"I... I don't know what my father told you," Josselyn had said, haltingly.

"He has told me the bare minimum," Cenzo had replied.

It was the first time she'd heard his voice. Low, dangerous, and spiked with that accent that whispered to her of European capitals and Italy's rolling hills. He made her shiver. Made her break out in goose bumps.

Made her wish she had already started running.

"I don't know what that means."

"Then I will tell you." Cenzo stayed where he was at the other end of the room, dominating the old fireplace. It was impossible not to notice how tall he was. How he commanded this space that had been her family's for generations. As if it was his. As if she was his. As if this was no more to him than going through the motions. "Your father, who was in another life my own father's roommate at Yale, has made me an intriguing proposition. And I have accepted it."

"Proposition?" she had repeated, her heart hammering in her chest. When she'd already known. When this had been inevitable all along. It was a wonder only that her father had not married her off before now, and how had she convinced herself that he had let go of that notion? She'd known full well her father was not in the habit of letting go. Of anything.

"We will marry, you and I," Cenzo told her. There had been something cruel in his gaze. In the elegant brutality that she could see all over his features, no matter that it was tempered with that sensuality beneath it. She had the thought that a knife could be dulled, but it was no less a knife. "It is your father's wish and I have chosen to grant it."

"Before even meeting me?" Josselyn had asked, feeling as if she was being daring when surely it was a reasonable enough question.

But Cenzo had smiled, that was what she remembered chiefly from that first day. That smile. It was as if he'd carved it down the length of her spine with the dullest knife in his possession.

"Meeting you is but a formality, *cara*," he had said. "Our wedding, now I have agreed to it, is a foregone conclusion."

Josselyn, despite a lifetime of having the necessity for good manners at all costs pounded into her, had turned on her heel and run. Not into the sea, only off toward the woods, a choice she would have a lot of time to regret.

Over the next year, she had spent entirely too much time remembering Cenzo's laugh as she'd run, chasing her from the room. Following her into sleep. Disturbing her wherever she went.

But her father had not been swayed by any arguments. He hardly acknowledged them, much less any talk of laughter. He had chosen Cenzo Falcone for his only daughter and that was an end to it.

Josselyn had assured herself that this time, she might defy him. This time she would stand up to him, because surely—though he had spent years telling her of his plans to assure her safety even after he was gone, and what he expected her to do—

he could not mean he truly expected her to marry a stranger.

But he did.

She had tried to comfort herself with the knowledge that while Cenzo was a stranger to *her*, their families had long been connected. Their fathers had been friends since university, and Archibald had spent time palling around with his friend and Cenzo's mother in places like giddy London and the South of France. Long before Archibald had married Josselyn's mother, then lost her. And before Cenzo's father had died, as well.

Archibald had told her these stories since she was a child. Surely, she thought that first year, the fact that she and the forbidding man she was to marry had both lost a parent should work in their favor. It should connect them, that enduring grief.

She'd convinced herself it would.

If she couldn't change her father's mind, it would.

A year later, she had met Cenzo once again.

This time, the occasion was their engagement party, to be held in a restaurant high in a Philadelphia skyscraper with views to die for and Michelin-starred food to tempt the well-heeled guests. Josselyn had not staged a protest, no matter how many times her friends offered to act as getaway drivers. She had been dressed and, she'd thought, prepared.

Her schemes to escape her fate had all ended in nothing, because her tragedy was that she understood her father. She knew why he wanted her to do this archaic thing. And she had never managed to mount a satisfactory rebellion because she cared too much about him to hurt him. It had been only the two of them for so long, and they were the only ones who knew what they'd lost. They were the only ones who still felt the ghosts of Mirabelle Byrd Christie and young Jack wherever they went.

Josselyn didn't have it in her to defy him. Not when all that was required of her was no more than had been asked of countless women through the centuries.

Including her own mother.

That was the argument that had worked the best. The one that had allayed a great many of her fears. Because Mirabelle had been nineteen when she'd become engaged to Archibald, twenty when she'd married him, and barely twenty-one when she'd had Jack. Her notably stern father, Bartholomew Byrd, had arranged the match himself. Mirabelle had famously sobbed on her wedding day and had locked herself in the bathroom of the fancy Philadelphia hotel that was the first stop on the couple's honeymoon later that night.

And yet despite such inauspicious beginnings, Josselyn's parents had fallen in love.

*Trust me*, her father had told Josselyn the morning of her engagement party. *All I want for you is what your mother and I had.*

And Josselyn had wanted that too. Really, she did, she'd decided. She'd taken care with her outfit, choosing a gown that she was certain could only please the implacable man she was to marry. Even if it did not, because men were nothing if not inscrutable, she felt confident it would look beautiful in all the society pages and her father would feel honored by her acquiescence. She had lectured herself, repeatedly, to remain openhearted. To trust in her father, as he'd asked, because surely he would never choose for her a man who was truly as harsh and inhuman as Cenzo seemed to be.

*Remember*, she had told herself, *you have that connection.*

She'd ordered herself to cast aside all the gossipy tidbits she'd collected about him over the past year. The many stunning and often famous ex-lovers, all of whom seemed broken when he finished with them. Broken, yet never spiteful, no matter how publicly he had tossed them aside. Josselyn knew too many things about him. A collection of details that together created an overwhelmingly ferocious mosaic and did nothing at all to calm her fears. Like his father before him, Cenzo had come to the States for his education, spending his formative years at Choate before going on to Yale. At Yale he had distinguished himself as a great intellect and excellent football player, then had gone on to Harvard Business School, where he parlayed a small fraction of his fortune into the beginnings of the multinational Fortune 500 company he had sold off five years back. For another fortune, and then some.

They claimed he'd done it simply to prove he could. That a man born with too many silver spoons to count had made his own.

Where Cenzo Falcone walked, the Italian papers liked to claim, the earth shook.

Josselyn had laughed at that in the privacy of her bedroom in her father's house. But she had not laughed when Cenzo had arrived that night to pick her up. For she was sure that she could feel the ground beneath her feet buckle when he strode inside.

He had studied her as if she was a bit of livestock on the auction block.

And despite herself, Josselyn had found that she was biting her tongue, hoping that he did not find her wanting.

Cenzo had not spoken. He was a vision of rampant masculinity, somehow elegant and breathtakingly ruthless at once. His evening clothes only seemed to call attention to the width of his shoulders, the narrowness of his hips, and the wide swathe of muscled chest in between. Most men of Josselyn's acquaintance looked somehow antiseptic in evening clothes, but not so Cenzo. He seemed to burn bright where he stood. He was alarmingly raw and shockingly vital, so that it was hard to look at him directly.

She'd had the unnerving notion that though this man might pretend that he was civilized, though his blood ran hot with the dawn of too many civilizations to count, he was not.

*He was not.*

A notion that was only compounded when he, still silent, came to take her hand.

Josselyn had frozen still, even though his touch had made a new, insistent heat roar through her. But it was good that she hadn't leaped away at his touch, because he was not caressing her or making advances. He was not holding her hand. He was sliding a ring into place.

"The ring has been in my family for too many generations to count," he had informed her, his ancient eyes gleaming with a light she could not have begun to read, though it made her skin prickle. "It is always worn by the bride of the eldest Falcone son and heir."

As if she lived in a cave and had never heard of the Sicilian Sky.

Standing in her wedding reception, Josselyn looked down at the famous deep blue diamond. It was a remarkable heirloom, passed down for centuries and possessed of its own myths. It had been stolen in the sixteenth century but recovered after much accusation and suffering. There had been duels to procure it, intrigue and backstabbing across generations. And it was no dainty, elegant ring. It looked like what it was. A twelve-carat stamp of ownership in the ornate setting it had enjoyed since the Industrial Revolution. The mark of the ferocious clan who had wrested power from almost every European government that had ever existed, yet had both lived and thrived.

It had fit Josselyn's finger perfectly.

Today, Cenzo had slid a deceptively simple band of gold onto her finger. His expression in the church had been grim. His eyes had glittered while his absurdly male jaw had been hard. His vows had fallen against her like threats.

But it was that band of gold that seemed to Josselyn to be made of concrete, even now. She looked down at her hand and it no longer looked like hers. Not with that blue diamond weighing down her hand. Not with that gold ring that declared her a wife.

*His* wife.

The music stopped playing and Josselyn looked up to see what was happening in this reception of hers. Only to find everyone looking at her with varying degrees of pity and speculation. She looked around to see Cenzo—her new husband, God help her—moving through the crowd that fell back to allow him through. Like a knife through butter.

Directly at her.

She told herself it was excitement. Hope. Even happiness. But the truth was that as he bore down upon her, a look of hard triumph on his face, Josselyn felt as if she was on the verge of a full-scale panic attack.

But she could not allow it, no matter how her heart pounded.

*Pull yourself together*, she ordered herself. She looked to the side, possibly in search of the nearest exit, but instead her gaze fell on her father. Archibald, beaming at what he saw before him. Filled with all the hope and happiness she couldn't feel herself.

Josselyn reminded herself, again, why it was she did this thing.

It was for the man who had raised her so gently in the wake of her mother's and brother's deaths. The man who had not fobbed her off to nannies or servants as she knew so many in his position would have.

The man who had dried her tears, who had held her and comforted her.

Now it was her turn. This was her chance to comfort him.

And so when Cenzo Falcone—the beautiful calamity she had married today and who might well be the end of her—stopped before her and extended his hand, Josselyn smiled. Brightly, as if this truly was the happiest day of her life.

Then she screwed up her courage and took it, letting him lead her away from all she'd ever known.

# CHAPTER TWO

Cenzo Falcone burned.

And his wife's hand in his had not helped matters any.

Hours later, high above the Atlantic in one of his fleet of private jets, he sat in his office while his palm yet stung. He flexed it, scowling down at his own flesh when what he wanted was to storm down the length of the plane and find her. And make her account for her unexpected effect on him.

Josselyn had politely excused herself not long after they'd taken off, eyes demurely downcast—no doubt to hide her skepticism of this whole enterprise, and he could not have said he blamed her—and Cenzo had let her go.

Graciously. Magnanimously.

Because she might as well get used to the fact that she was his wife before he showed her what their marriage would entail.

That same old roaring thing in him stirred anew.

Cenzo called it his dragon. The beast that lived in him and had done since his father had taken his own life. The creature that roared and spouted fire, clawed and fought, and had led him here at last. To Archibald Christie and the one and only thing he held dear.

*My daughter is my one true treasure*, the old man had said when he'd had the temerity to contact Cenzo. When he had seemed wholly unaware of the damage his inattention had done when it mattered most. *I hope I can entrust her to your care.*

And Cenzo had known his duty as a Falcone—the last Falcone in his branch of the ancient family—from a very young age. Regardless of his feelings on the subject, he knew that he must marry. It was up to him to continue the bloodline. To make certain that the Falcone legacy did not end with him, nor get shunted off to one of the distant cousins his mother always called *those circling vultures* no matter how obsequious they were.

Still, he had always assumed that he would do that particular duty…later.

Much later.

But when Archibald Christie had made his astonishing offer, there was not one single part of Cenzo that could refuse it. Because it was immediately clear to him that there could be only one thing better than taking out his revenge on the old man who deserved whatever he got, and it was this.

He would destroy the daughter instead, and make Archibald live with *that* for the rest of his miserable life.

A task that he would have set himself to with the same intensity no matter the circumstances, but one that had taken on a different shape since the day he'd actually met the daughter in question. He had seen any number of pictures. Once he had agreed to come to Archibald in his remote summer retreat in deepest Maine, Cenzo had studied up on the girl. He wanted to know everything about her. He wanted to learn her inside and out.

Because the more he knew, the more he could use it against her.

And against her vile father.

He had seen from the pictures that she was lovely. Lovelier than the daughter of his enemy had any right to be, he had thought when he'd seen the first round of photographs. And far more attractive than those bloodless Americans usually were, always swanning around so enamored of their history when it amounted to very little in the grand scheme of things. Cenzo could trace his family to the Holy Roman Empire. What was anything American but a blink of an eye next to that?

What he had not been prepared for was the reality of his enemy's daughter, standing there looking like some kind of beach bum that day in Maine. Unstudied. Artless. He had expected her to vamp a bit.

To make at least some attempt to flirt with him, for that was what women did when they found themselves alone with the great Cenzo Falcone.

Instead, Josselyn Christie had looked at him as if he defied understanding—and not in the way he usually did, by simple virtue of being himself—and had run.

It had troubled him all throughout the following year as he'd set about making his arrangements and, far more daunting, preparing his embittered mother to accept what must happen. He had pored through the reports his people delivered on Josselyn, looking for scandals. Anything to shift the balance, to make the daughter at least as compromised as her father, and best of all—to give him ammunition.

He did not care to ask himself why he, Cenzo Falcone, required *ammunition* to deal with a poor little heiress being sold into his keeping.

And in any case, there was nothing.

There was only the stain of her, seeped deep into his skin, surprising him at the strangest moments.

Then came their engagement party, when he had bestowed upon her the Sicilian Sky that he had only before then seen gracing his own mother's hand. The stone that had caused as much trouble as it ever had joy. More, perhaps. Such was the weight of history.

*But what purpose is there in joy,* his father had liked to say, *if it does not carry with it the weight of sorrow? You cannot have one without the other,* mio figlio. *They only make sense when they are fused together into one.*

His mother had always been the more severe of his parents, and rarely worried herself overmuch about the unlikely appearance of any joy. Though Cenzo knew that Françoise Falcone did not consider herself dour so much as realistic—and French.

And since her husband's death, the Widow Falcone had also felt that it was her sacred duty to protect the Falcone name—and interests—at any cost. She had not wished to hand over the ring to an upstart American, no matter what Cenzo planned to do with her.

*The stone is worth a fortune or two, certainly*, Françoise had said, back when it was valued for a mere fifty-five million euros. *But its true value is that others covet it. And the more they covet it, the shinier it seems. This has always been so. The myth of it makes it far more valuable than any mere piece of jewelry.*

And she had always made it clear that while not every woman had risen to the occasion of wearing such an iconic heirloom throughout its storied history, *she* did not intend to fall beneath its weight. Nor had she. She had still worn it years after Cenzo's father had died, spine straight and tall, her eyes forever trained on the glory of the Falcone name. And had required no little coaxing to relinquish it when Cenzo had asked, though she had claimed that had everything to do with its intended new recipient and nothing at all to do with the fact she'd grown to consider it truly hers.

*The ring is only ever on loan, Maman,* Cenzo had murmured. *It can never truly belong to anyone.*

She had shaken with the force of her distaste. *It is the chain of custody that I find objectionable. And perverse.*

He had not had to remind her that the ring was his by rights, and had been since his father had drawn his final breath. He had not needed to.

And he had resented how it looked on Josselyn's finger, how it caught a new light. He had more than resented it—he'd told himself he had actively disliked it. That it was *dislike* that had moved in him, forging a new path of fire.

What else could it have been?

But now he was suspended between the moon and the vast ocean below, and he was not a liar. Not even to himself. Not ever. He might have pretended there in the foyer of her father's house, because the ring on her finger had disconcerted him. He was too attuned to its history, perhaps. He was too aware of the things that tended to happen when the ring changed hands. Wars and ruin, horror and shame…though not in recent centuries.

He had lied and told himself that his reaction was nothing but distaste for the task before him, however necessary. But the engagement party had told him the truth. There had been dancing, because there was always dancing at these things no matter what year it was. Old formalities never died. And because it was expected, he had led his fiancée to the floor so that other wealthy people could gawp at them.

A public service, he had told himself, as none of the guests were the sort who liked to read the society pages to see things they believed they ought to have witnessed in person.

That night, Josselyn's dark hair had been glossy, caught up at the nape of her neck in something quietly elegant—complicated enough to suggest a bit of drama without actually committing to it. Her dress had been a revelation after the beach clothes he'd seen her in before. There was no disguising her figure in the gown she'd chosen, a sweep of red held at one shoulder by a clasp of sparkling jewels.

He had found himself unduly obsessed with the mark near her lips that should have made her flawed, to his mind. But instead it did the opposite. It was as if her one slight imperfection made everything else more perfect, not less.

And Cenzo did not wish to think of this woman as *perfect* in any regard. Everything in him had rebelled. He had ordered himself to walk away from her, there in the middle of their engagement party, surrounded by the sort of empty, overly fatuous society people he detested. No matter their country of origin.

But instead, he danced with her, because he was playing a long game. He had held her close, so close that he'd been able to identify the scent she wore—a whisper of something like citrus with deeper notes that reminded him of the sea.

They had not spoken. He'd had nothing to say. And Josselyn had looked at him as if he were part monster, part dream. Cenzo had told himself that she saw the dragon in him, that was all.

Maybe he only hoped she might.

And he had spent another year attempting to come to terms with the odd…complications he'd felt that night. The need in him, when he did not wish to feel such sensations where she was concerned. It made things easier that he wanted her, he could admit that, but he did not wish to want her to the extent he did.

It was sheer lust, if he was truthful. And it didn't make sense. His object had always been perfectly clear when it came to the Christies. When he had been younger, he'd focused more intently on Archibald as the obvious architect of his father's untimely end. But it had been clear to him, ever since that very first, astonishing call when Archibald had dared to suggest marriage, that the daughter was the better target.

Because what he did to Josselyn would hurt her, but it would kill her father—yet let him live with it.

*Lusting* for her seemed to fly in the face of all he intended to accomplish.

Accordingly he'd spent this last year digging even deeper into what made Josselyn Christie tick.

Like him, she had gone to an American East Coast boarding school. After she graduated, she and some friends had taken the summer to wander aimlessly through winter in Australia and New Zealand. In the fall, she had returned to follow her family's tradition, on the women's side, and started at Vassar. Cenzo had found no indication that she had been any more scandalous there than any other coed. The odd parties, a cringeworthy attempt at black box theater, a semester abroad in Italy. She had lived on campus all four years and had maintained the same group of close friends, all of whom had attended their wedding today.

After college, she had spent another summer traveling, this time in Europe. When she'd returned, she had moved back in to her childhood home, and as far as he could tell, had done nothing but serve the interests of her father ever since.

There were no deep, dark secrets to dig up. He would have found them. And in many ways, that was a good thing. Because it meant the focus could be entirely, deservedly, on Archibald's sins.

He thought now, staring out the window at the

darkness beyond and the moon above, that he was going to take great pleasure in showing her exactly who her father really was.

"I will avenge you, Patri," he said quietly, using the same words he always used. The vow as much a part of him as his own bones. His own flesh. "I will make them pay."

Cenzo did not sleep, for he had waited far too long. A lifetime, it seemed, though he knew full well his father had only quit this life some fifteen years before.

*Promise me*, his mother had said before he had left to make this trip to America. His final trip, to collect his bride and bring her home at last. *Promise me that no matter what else happens, you will not forget who you are. What these people have done to you. To me. And most of all, to your father.*

*How do you imagine I could ever forget?* Cenzo had asked.

Françoise Falcone was not a happy woman. This was forever evident in her face, for all that she was very beautiful. There was always that sternness. That coldness. He liked to think it had been put there since they'd lost his father, but he knew that was not so. She had never been warm.

And still, the way she had looked at him then had chilled him.

*Young women have their ways*, she had told him, her tone dark. Her gaze had fixed on him as if he had already betrayed her. *Their wiles. It may be, my son, that you believe yourself to be the hunter when it is you who are the prey.*

Cenzo had laughed.

But then he had stood at the head of the church aisle and watched the woman who would become his wife move toward him, a vision in white. She had looked serene, her face a perfect oval, marred only by that beauty mark that was no flaw at all.

Her touch had warmed him, but he should not have cared about such things. About biology. He had held her hands in his, said the ancient words in English, and now he wore the ring that she had placed on his finger in her turn. He could not get used to it.

He looked at it now, gleaming in the light of the plane. He could not get used to any of this.

Cenzo did not wish to react to this woman. He wished only to use her for his own ends.

And he vowed, yet again, that would be so.

Because he was Cenzo Falcone. What he wanted was his, one way or another.

It was still dark outside as the plane began its descent into Sicily. He left his office, moving out into the common area of the jet, and was somehow unsurprised to find his bride already waiting there. He eyed her critically as he approached the sitting area, the jet's many hints of gold making her seem to gleam.

Once again, she was a new version of the woman

he knew so many details about—yet still did not know at all.

Today she did not wear her wedding gown, of course. And as he registered that, Cenzo had a brief, horrifying pang of need. Sharp and alarming, because it wasn't the simple lust he had tried to come to terms with already. He understood that though he had never considered himself sentimental, he found himself wishing he might have taken the traditional role of removing that flowing white dress from her slender body. To see, after two years of wondering, if her breasts were as plush and high as they looked. Because, like it or not, he had spent a remarkable amount of time considering the flare of her hips and wondering how they would feel in his hands while he drove himself inside her.

Soon enough, he told himself. Soon enough.

He took the seat opposite Josselyn, letting his gaze fall where it would. She'd chosen to wear a deceptively simple outfit to begin her life as his wife. A sweater, a pair of jeans, low-heeled short boots. An outfit that should have been unremarkable, but for the excellence of the pieces she'd chosen. The drape of the fabric, the heft, the rich camel leather of her boots—it all spoke of understated elegance and impressive wealth. She wore diamonds in her ears—small, yet of high quality. There was a delicate chain around her neck, a faint glimpse of gold, because she did not need to be flashy.

Especially not when she wore the Sicilian Sky on her finger, elevating her sartorial choices to high art.

Cenzo told himself that he was gathering information, that was all, and there was no need for the immediate response in his sex. There had been the beach bum he'd met first, her hair wild and her clothes soft with age. He had imagined that version of her was the real one, untutored and unaware that he had been coming to call. As for their engagement party and their wedding, he had assumed that stylists had intervened—because the weddings of heiresses were not simple family affairs, and certainly not when he was involved. There had been extensive press coverage. He had imagined steps had been taken to tame her, to contain her, to make her fit the expected mold.

But it seemed he'd been wrong.

And that sensation was so rare that it took Cenzo some moments to place it. He was not often wrong. To his knowledge, he had never been wrong, in point of fact. But his bride—his *wife*—could have worn anything now that they were alone. And she had chosen a rather well-armored, well-conceived look to face any eventuality. Even if he'd been tempted to assume that her choices had been made for her by the same army of stylists he'd imagined had handled her at events thus far, that wouldn't explain her hair. She had taken it down, washed it, and had to have styled it herself, for there was no staff on the plane. It looked perfect, like the rest of her.

Meaning this was her natural state. Or her preferred defense.

He was forced to admire it.

And then told himself that was as well, because it could only benefit him if it turned out that she was a worthy adversary.

In and out of the marital bed.

"You have not told me where we are headed," Josselyn said into the taut silence, sounding perfectly calm and at her ease. As if she often found herself flying off into the unknown, married to a stranger.

"I have not," he agreed.

And then he lounged there, letting the moment drag out.

All Josselyn did was blink. There was no other outward sign of reaction. He filed that away.

"I see. Do you intend to let me in on the secret? Or is it to be a surprise? I was told only to bring my passport."

Cenzo eyed her, still looking for flaws. "This feels a bit like a bait and switch. I don't recall you saying a single word to me before now unless prompted by a priest, and now it is as if you are made of demands. Is this what I can expect from my wife?"

She sat straighter and he realized that her posture, too, added to the overall sense of her elegance. Even without the Sicilian Sky on her hand, her poise alone would have shouted out that she was a woman to be reckoned with.

It really was such a shame that he could not simply admire her.

"There has been no opportunity for conversation until now." Josselyn's voice was as serene as she looked. Yet with a hint of steel beneath, which pleased him. "At our first meeting, I will admit, I felt overwhelmed by the decision you and my father had made. Appropriately, I think. We only met one other time before yesterday and as I recall, you spent most of our time alone engaged in a series of business calls."

"Is that a complaint?"

"Not even remotely." She smiled the same smile he'd seen her flash all over the place on two occasions now, all good manners and vast, unbridgeable distances. "I am only offering you an accounting of our interactions. From my perspective."

"It is all the same to me, *cara*. If you wish to fight. If you wish to make demands. If you fling yourself prostrate and attempt to impress me with a show of submissiveness. None of that will change what is to happen."

Her face brightened. She folded her hands before her and placed them on the little table that separated them, the huge stone on her finger making light bounce all around them. "Wonderful. There's an agenda. I can't wait to hear it."

Cenzo laughed. "Truly, you are like a lamb to the slaughter."

Her polite smile cooled, but only by a degree. "Surely there will be no need for slaughtering of any kind. This is a marriage, not an abattoir."

Josselyn waited, clearly offering him the opportunity to leap in and explain himself. He declined it.

"I think it might serve us both well if we lay out our expectations," she said after a moment. And while her smile did not dim, her voice sounded more…careful. "We're lucky, really. No need to be encumbered by romantic notions. No need to hope and pray that love wins the day. We can civilly decide, you and I, what our life together will be in a way that people in our generation rarely do. I find myself quite optimistic."

He only laughed. For longer, this time.

But his wife did not crumble. She kept that smile on her face and did not seem to tense so much as a stray muscle. It was impressive.

Or would have been, had he allowed himself to find her impressive.

Josselyn's gaze was level on his. "If you will not share what you wish to get out of our marriage, perhaps you might share the source of your amusement. Or is the aim to laugh mysteriously, and alone, for the rest of our days?"

Cenzo regarded her, doing nothing to wash away the laughter he was sure was still stamped all over his face. "Why do you suppose your father bartered you away in marriage to a stranger?"

He thought he saw emotion in her gaze, but she blinked it away. "You are not a stranger to him. Only to me."

"I suppose that is true, though he had not seen me since I was a boy. It was my late father that he knew."

And she could not know how those words cost him. When Archibald Christie had done so much more than simply *know* his father. But he kept his dragon in check. It wasn't time, yet, to let his fury take hold.

"In any case, it is not as if he chose you off the street," Josselyn said. "But he did choose you deliberately. And he did this because my father is of an old school. He believes that money and power are the only things that could possibly keep me safe in this world."

"You must agree with him, then. To have accepted this arrangement."

"It's funny," she said, though she wasn't laughing, "but I thought these were the sorts of conversations we should have had at any point over the past two years."

Cenzo lifted a careless shoulder. "We are having the conversation now."

"Whether I agree with him or not doesn't matter, because I decided—" and he was certain there was an emphasis on that word *decided* "—to acquiesce to his wishes for me."

"Convenient, then, that his wishes for you have made you one of the wealthiest women in the world. Overnight."

It was Josselyn's turn to shrug. Hers was delicate, yet no less dismissive. "As he has quite a bit of money and power himself, I expect my father looked around for one of the few men he believes has more."

"You make it sound like a fairy tale," Cenzo murmured. "The dutiful, obedient daughter who does as her father wishes no matter the cost. But I'm afraid, *cara*, that your father has made a terrible mistake."

Josselyn did not react. Which, he supposed, was itself a reaction. "What do you mean? What mistake?"

"I did not know if I would tell you this." He was enjoying himself, now. "Your father seemed to have no notion of what he'd done. It was perhaps unsurprising that you would not, either. I will confess that at first, I didn't believe it."

"I have absolutely no idea what you're talking about."

"And for some while I've thought it would be amusing to have you figure it out as we went." Cenzo smiled then and did nothing to make it more palatable. Less edgy or dark. "But you see, simply punishing you for your father's sins would not be enough."

"Punish me?" She shook her head, making her hair move. And he could smell the sea once more, sweet and crisp. Inviting, damn her. "Why on earth would I require punishment? Or my father, of all people? He has his flaws, like anyone, but he is a good man at heart."

"No." Cenzo bit out the word. "He is not."

Josselyn laughed then. "You must be joking. He's set in his ways, sure. He's a product of his generation. He has some very outdated ideas and believes too much in his own discernment, sometimes to his detriment. But he's not *evil*."

And he could not tell, in that moment, if he regretted going down this path. Perhaps he should have done as originally planned and let her parse it out over the coming month, assuming she had the faculties to do such a thing. He did not intend to give her much room or time to *think*. Maybe he should have kept her in suspense. That had been his intention.

But she was too perfect. She seemed less a tool to him now and more an actual opponent.

He had not been able to resist.

That was on him. But when it came to the terms of what would happen between them, there could be no equivocation.

"You may feel a sense of daughterly obligation," Cenzo said, his voice low and his gaze a bright fury on hers. "I suppose that is to your credit. But it is misplaced."

"But you like my father," she protested, her eyes widening. "You spent time with him. He told me he'd thoroughly vetted you and furthermore, enjoyed the time he spent with you. He said that you reminded him of your father."

"The rantings of a guilty conscience and nothing more."

"Guilty?" Josselyn frowned at him. "Of what?"

"I'm glad you asked," Cenzo growled at her, and knew in that moment that this was the right course of action. Because it felt like a relief. "Your father might not have driven the car as it went over that cliff, but he killed my father all the same."

# CHAPTER THREE

JOSSELYN FELT AS if Cenzo had driven the two of them over the side of a towering mountain. Some part of her, in a sudden rush of madness, almost wished that he had.

Because she'd spent her wedding night alone, and she had chosen to view that as consideration on his part. As a sign of respect. *He's giving you space*, she'd told herself. He might have been overwhelming and intense in every regard, but this marriage of theirs would be fine if it started that way. On such rational, reasonable footing. She'd assured herself of that, again and again.

She had curled up in a ball on the bed in her stateroom and had chanted that to herself as she tried to sleep. Over and over as the jet flew through the dark.

*This marriage will be fine.*

Finding herself confronted with the news that this marriage was not only not going to be fine, but that he had been *plotting revenge* all the while, was jarring.

More than jarring. Josselyn felt winded.

"I don't understand," she managed to say after a few moments. She was doing her best to present a calm, impenetrable surface, the way she'd learned long ago. It was the best way to handle excitable men who believed deeply that they were anything but. Normally her own serene facade made her feel better, but not today. It did nothing to keep her heart from catapulting itself against her ribs. Still, she refused to give in to the panic that rose inside her. "You worked out the details with my father yourself. Why would you do that if you thought that he was involved with what happened?"

Cenzo laughed, but it was a terrible sound. Mocking. Dark. It curled inside of her and made her bones feel cold. "Archibald Christie was not *involved* in what happened to my father. He *is* what happened to my father."

Josselyn wanted to leap to her feet. She wanted to put as much distance as possible between herself and this conversation. She wanted to escape… whatever this was.

But she was on a private jet. There was nowhere to go. And even the small protection of her stateroom wouldn't help her now, because they were landing. Even bouncing a little on the tarmac as if in tune with his laughter.

It took everything she had to stay put. To keep her panic from her face. She wasn't sure she succeeded.

"There were any number of ways I could have made your father pay," Cenzo told her as the plane taxied on a dark runway, with only a few lights in the distance to make it clear they weren't still in the air. He sounded as if he was *confiding* in her. And as if the act brought him great pleasure. "I chose the one calculated to hurt him the most."

"How lovely," Josselyn managed to say, through lips that felt frozen. She kept her gaze on him, though the cabin lights had gone dark. That did nothing to dim those ancient eyes of his, blazing straight at her. "Here I thought that despite the archaic nature of our situation, we might be able to work together to come up with the kind of union that benefited us both. Since we both agreed to do this."

"There will be a great benefit, I assure you." Cenzo laughed again. He looked entirely at his ease. "But the benefit will be mine."

It took her a breath, maybe two, to realize through the tumult inside her that the plane itself had stopped. Cenzo did not move. He continued to lounge there across from her as if he was an ancient emperor preparing to order an execution. And it was as if everything inside Josselyn shivered to a humming sort of halt, waiting for that gesture that would decide her fate. Desperate for any hint of compassion in his gaze when there was none.

But the jet door was thrown open then, and Josselyn told herself it felt like a gift. Even if, somewhere beneath the relief, there was a part of her that almost resented the interruption. Because she wanted to *do* something. Make a stand. Refuse to exit the plane when Cenzo stood, then beckoned for her to precede him down the stairs with exaggerated courtesy. But she didn't see the point in a protest. Not now, when she didn't even know where they were.

*Or perhaps you worry that he would simply bodily remove you himself,* a voice inside her countered. *And what do you think you would do with his hands upon you?*

She repressed the shiver that notion caused. She repressed it so hard it almost hurt.

And either way, Josselyn walked down the stairs herself, stepping out into a thick night. Once she made it down to the tarmac she paused, trying to figure out where they were. Her location seemed far more critical in that moment than…the peril shaped like a man who prowled down the stairs after her. The air was more sultry here. Back in Pennsylvania it had still been warm, but there were hints of the coming fall in the September mornings. Whispers in the wind at night. Here she could smell nothing of fall. There were flowers on the breeze, and a rich salt that told her she was near the sea. The very dark around her seemed secretive, whispering things she couldn't quite understand.

Josselyn accepted that she was being fanciful. And fanciful wasn't going to help her. Nothing was.

*You married him,* her trusty voice within condemned her.

As if she might have forgotten that part, with what passed for the Crown Jewels on her hand.

Not to mention the terrifying man who had given it to her.

Cenzo appeared beside her and gripped her elbow with a possessiveness that would have stolen her breath even if she wasn't already so...undone. And there was a moment, a breath, where he looked down upon her from his great height and Josselyn wondered if she might do as everything screamed in her to do, tear her elbow from his grasp, and run for it.

But that would be giving him what he wanted. She understood that implicitly. He wanted her reaction. He wanted some acknowledgment that whatever game he was playing here, it was working.

Josselyn decided she would rather die where she stood than give it to him. So all she did was smile coolly, remaining as outwardly serene as she could.

Something she would continue to do unless and until it killed her.

Cenzo handed her into the front passenger seat of a rugged sort of SUV, then rounded the hood and swung into the driver's seat. Josselyn was surprised. She would have assumed his tastes ran to sports cars like crotch rockets, not hardy vehicles with four-wheel drive. He did not spare her a glance— another gift, she told herself stoutly—as he drove into the dark as if he knew it well.

Josselyn clutched at the handle beside her, not exactly shocked to discover that Cenzo Falcone drove too fast. As if his expectation was that the narrow road would arrange itself before him to best suit him. It irritated her that, as far as she could tell, it did.

She focused out the window, where his headlights picked up groves of almond trees, tangles of bougainvillea, and a rocky coastline that flirted with the sea.

"You've brought me home to Sicily," Josselyn said into the dark tension between them. "You could have just said so."

In the distance, the sky began to lighten. The first sign yet that the sun was soon to rise.

Maybe it was foolish that she clung to that notion as if it meant that there was hope.

"To Sicily, yes," Cenzo replied. Though he took his time with it. "But not home. I have something else in mind for you, *mia moglie*."

*My wife.* It was truly something how he made that sound like an insult.

"How wonderful," Josselyn said smoothly. "I can't wait."

And that same mocking laughter of his seemed to draw tight around her, like a noose.

He drove her down to a rocky cove, where a boat waited. He ushered her on board, and Josselyn supposed she ought to have been grateful that it wasn't a tiny little outboard motor, barely more than a skiff. It was a much larger, sturdier sort of fishing boat, with a cabin below and a deck to shield passengers from wind and waves. She stood as near to the bow as she could get without stepping back out into the early morning breeze. And she gripped her hands tight together to keep herself from screaming while Cenzo and his crew had what was clearly a riotously amusing conversation in Italian. All of them speaking far too quickly for her to pick up much more than a few words in the Italian she'd last used during her semester abroad in Rome.

Another set of headlights came down to the cove, and Josselyn watched as luggage was loaded onto the boat. Her luggage as well as a set of cases that she had last seen in Pennsylvania, and so knew belonged to Cenzo.

Another sign that boded ill, she had to think.

Once again, it was almost a relief when the boat set off, moving slowly from the cove and then picking up speed as it left the land behind.

"When will you tell me what it is you plan to

do with me?" Josselyn asked when Cenzo came to stand beside her, though she kept her gaze trained on the dark waves and the ever-brightening sky. It was pinkening to the east, water and sky alike. "Or is the mystery part of your fun?"

She felt that impossible stare of his on the side of her face, but she did not look at him. Because she was certain that was what he wanted her to do. And hers might be a soft and pointless rebellion. Josselyn accepted that. But it was all she had at the moment, so she leaned into it.

"I'm not going to toss you overboard, if that is your fear." Cenzo, by contrast, continued to sound more and more amused.

"I'm delighted to hear it," Josselyn said crisply. "But there's a lot of room between being forced to walk the proverbial plank and the civil, polite marriage I thought we'd agreed to. You can see how a reasonable person might doubt your motives."

"When did we make such an agreement? You appear to have all manner of notions about this agreement you say we made when I cannot recall ever discussing the particulars of our marriage." He laughed. "Not with you, *cara.*"

She wanted, very badly, to tell him not to call her that. But suspected that whatever else he might choose to call her was worse than any ubiquitous endearment.

"I think you know that my father would never

have agreed to anything that might hurt me. Like, for example, a revenge plot." She squeezed her fingers more tightly together as the boat bounced across the waves, and she liked that it wasn't comfortable to do that any longer. Not with that enormous ring cutting into her flesh. Because the discomfort grounded her, somehow. It made it matter less that she was on a boat somewhere in the Mediterranean with her brand-new husband and his *plots*. "I must assume that you misrepresented yourself."

"I did what was necessary."

She looked at him then, the precarious dawn seeming to call attention to the stark lines of his face. Cruel and yet still beautiful, even now that she knew better. "We are agreed, then. You're a liar."

A corner of his hard, sensual mouth kicked up. "You may call me whatever you wish, Josselyn. It will not change a thing."

"So what is it to be?" she demanded, with a grand sort of sweeping bravado she in no way felt. "Will you lock me away in some tower? Will I be put in jail for the supposed sins of my father? Or do you intend to abuse me yourself?"

Cenzo studied her face while around them, the world got brighter. His gaze did not.

He lifted a hand and Josselyn braced herself, everything in her spinning wildly. Did he truly plan to strike her? What would she *do*?

Was this really happening?

But he did not land any blow. He reached over and traced her cheekbone with a careless finger, moving it down after a lazy sort of sketch to find her beauty mark.

Just that odd little touch, then he dropped his hand.

And Josselyn felt the same great tumult she always did where he was concerned. Panic and longing, and that terrible heat.

Too much heat.

She was glad it was still dark enough that, if she was lucky, he would not see all the ways her body reacted to him. Josselyn wasn't sure she could bear the shame.

What had seemed hopeful yesterday—that attraction, that fire, between a bride and groom who hardly knew each other—seemed like nothing but a betrayal now.

"I will not have to abuse you," he told her softly. Much too softly, when the look on his face was enigmatic. And made the blood in her veins seem to run hot and soft, like syrup. "For one thing, I have no taste for such things. I'm not a monster."

"Are you not?" she bit out, though her cheek still felt as if he had lit her on fire.

Again, a tug of his lips. "You might wish that I was a monster. That might bring you clarity, I suppose. But what I intend to be to you is far worse."

Deep inside her, Josselyn felt a kind of trembling. It wasn't fear. It was where the fear went, what it turned into. It was years of tamping down her feelings and putting herself last. Always so understanding of her father's needs, and his losses— far greater than hers. For it was true that she had lost her brother and her mother, but there was nothing worse than losing a child. And the love of one's life, all at once.

He had never made that argument. Josselyn had made it on his behalf.

She could hear her friends' voices in her ears, begging her to reconsider this marriage. Just as they had begged her over the years to gain some measure of independence from her father. To think of herself for a change. To build a life of her own.

But Josselyn had always taken comfort in the fact that her father cared for her. Truly he did. He was not vicious or cruel or even dismissive. He truly believed that what he was doing was the best for her, because he loved her. Just as she loved him. So she had held her tongue. She had let things go. She had never, ever showed him her true feelings about things unless her feelings aligned with his. What would be the point?

All of those choices bubbled up inside her now.

It was temper. And it was volcanic.

And she couldn't think of a better recipient than this man beside her. Her husband, whether she liked it or not.

"So far," she said, her voice harder than it had been in years—or possibly ever—"all you are to me is a duty to my father. And now, having acquitted that duty to the best of my abilities, this sounds like nothing but empty threats. Am I meant to be afraid that a man I care nothing about might harbor conspiracy theories? Why on earth would I care?"

Cenzo, apparently, did not realize that even so civilized a volcanic eruption from Josselyn was nothing less than a sea change. All he did was laugh again. "It seems you do have some fire within. I doubted it."

Temper kicked its way through her, making her think she might actually combust where she stood. "You do know that whatever it is you're planning, it cannot last, don't you? Whether you leave me on a raft in the middle of the sea, beat me black and blue, or merely lock me up somewhere, it will all end the same way. Sooner or later, my father will demand to see me. And then what will you do? Do you imagine that I will not tell him each and every indignity you make me suffer in the interim?"

"But that is the point," Cenzo said silkily. "I want you to tell him."

Josselyn felt her heart stutter a bit at that. The waves grew choppy, so she had to reach out and hold on to keep from being rocked off her feet. She noticed that Cenzo did not hold on to anything, and she instantly felt as if she'd lost any higher ground she might have gained by proving herself weaker.

But she ignored all that and focused on him instead. "Or we could fast-forward to the part where I tell him you're a terrible person, then file for divorce. Why all the theatrics?"

"I had a great many conversations with your father," Cenzo told her, and if she wasn't mistaken he sounded something like…satisfied. Her belly twisted into a knot. "Once I understood that you would obey him, there was no need to repeat those conversations with you. And I feel confident that your father does not believe in divorce. I should warn you, Josselyn, that neither do I."

It was a bit late for warnings, she thought. "Maybe not. But he also doesn't believe that I should be harmed. I think you'll find that his number one object in life is to make certain that I am never, ever, hurt in any way."

"I will not be 'beating you black and blue,' as you put it," Cenzo replied, as if she was the one who had said something distasteful. "I do not have to resort to brute force. I will not have to take you apart, *cara*. You will do it for me."

The boat, having picked up speed on the choppy water, began to slow. And Josselyn was more grateful than she wanted to admit that there was an excuse to look away from him. So quickly that it took her a moment or two to take in the island before her.

Though *island* seemed an exaggeration. It was a small bit of land, really more of a barren rock, and the only thing upon it was an ancient castle that rose up from the sea. More than half of it in ruins.

"You can't be serious," she said, hardly realizing she spoke out loud.

"Welcome to the Castello dei Sospiri," Cenzo said from beside her, sounding triumphant. And something far darker than that. "You would call it the Castle of Sighs. It was built as a fortress many centuries ago to keep invaders at bay. But not long after the Normans came it was converted to its current purpose, which is to serve as a kind of retreat for members of my family."

"A retreat," Josselyn repeated, scowling up at the unwelcoming old rocks before her. "Really."

There were stairs hewn into stone, leading up from the water. A great many stairs marching up toward the ruins. At the waterline there was nothing like a beach. There were rocks and a kind of jetty, a forlorn-looking dinghy hauled above the high tide mark, and what looked like a very rudimentary sailboat.

Dawn was breaking, painting the sky with gold and pink, and even that failed to make the castle before her look anything but lonely. Isolated.

*Dangerous*, something in her whispered. As if she needed the reminder.

Cenzo gazed up at it as if it was Buckingham Palace. "It is many a Falcone over the centuries who has been sent to this castle to rethink. Redirect. Relearn some things, even."

Her heart kicked at her wildly. "What you're saying is that this is a prison."

"Precisely." He smiled down at her then, those arresting eyes of his all the more breathtaking with the sunrise in them. "The world as you know it does not exist here. There are no servants, no staff. No mobile phone service. No internet. All such things are back on the mainland. When this boat leaves us here, it will not return for a month."

"A month?" Josselyn repeated, her voice beginning to sound thready. She cleared her throat. "That doesn't sound safe. What if, to pick a possibility at random, you woke up one morning to find you'd been justly stabbed in your sleep?"

"How delightfully bloodthirsty, Josselyn," he murmured, and she got the sense that he approved. "This obviously will not occur, if only because I do not intend to give you access to any sharp blades. But there is, naturally, a radio for emergencies."

"I thought you were supposed to be the most powerful and important man alive," she said, desperately trying to make sense of her predicament. Why was he doing…whatever he was doing? And exactly how prison-like was this going to be? "How will you continue to convince the world that's the case if they can't access you for a month? I thought men like you couldn't go without business calls for more than fifteen minutes at a time. Surely you'll crumble to ash if you're not buying or selling something."

"For you, Josselyn, I have cleared my schedule." When she only stared back at him, nonplussed, he laughed again. "It is our honeymoon, is it not? And you are a beautiful woman. Surely it cannot surprise you that I have set aside the whole world that I might enjoy the spoils I have gone to such lengths to claim."

"Wait. Is this… Is this a sex thing?" She shook her head, but she couldn't make sense of any of this. "You've got to be kidding me."

His laugh changed, then. It sounded like less of a weapon, and more like something real. And that wasn't any better.

Josselyn told herself that what slid down her spine, like a lick of naked flame, was fear. Or fury. Or both, fused together into a molten hot reaction that made her nipples tighten.

Because she refused to let it be anything else.

"I do not kid," he told her, almost gently. "Nothing will happen on this island unless you beg for it. Know that now. I told you I am not a monster, and I am not. I do not intend to take what will be so freely given."

*Arrogant*, she thought then, was really not a

strong enough word to describe this man. It didn't come close to the reality that was Cenzo Falcone.

"If you really wanted me to give you anything," she managed to grit out from between her clenched teeth, as the boat docked on the small outthrust bit of jetty that looked like it was only available at low tide, "anything at all, you've played your hand all wrong."

"I can assure you that I only play to win." He moved then, and she found herself turning her body as if to follow him. As if her body simply *wanted* to follow him. As if he was a magnet and she was helpless before the pull of him. "I want you to know, at every moment, exactly what is happening to you."

"But I don't—"

And then his hand was on her face, his hard fingers gripping her chin.

Cenzo tilted her face to his and kissed her.

It was a bruising, punishing kiss that she was shocked to find packed that same punch. That same delirious heat flooded through her, and it was not fear. It was nothing at all like fear, and it pooled between her legs like a new pulse.

When he lifted his head, Cenzo did not release her chin. And she could see from the expression on his hard face he knew.

*He knew.*

"In a month's time, we will leave here," he told her, his voice a rasp that seemed to do the same things in her that his kiss had. "And you will be my slave. Not because I make it so in some show of strength, Josselyn. But because you will beg me for the role. In my bed, of course. But everywhere else, too, because that is how much you will want me."

"You're delusional," she gasped, as something in her roared.

Again, not in fear.

That was more alarming than anything he'd done or said. Josselyn shoved herself back from him, jerking her chin out of his grasp. And found herself chastened at once, because even though she managed to put space between them, she was far too aware that he'd let her go.

"I knew from the moment we met how this would go," Cenzo said, his gaze so intense it hurt. It actually hurt. "It is inevitable. You should have lost your innocence while you had the chance, Josselyn. For I will shatter it, hoard it, and make it my own. And you will thank me for the privilege."

"And this is…" It seemed as if her heart was literally in her throat, trying to pound its way out of her body. "Do you truly believe that somehow, breaking me down in this fashion is revenge?"

"Josselyn. *Cara.* What is it your father wants for you most of all?" But he didn't wait for her to answer. His ancient eyes were aglow. His cruel face was too beautiful to bear. "He wants you safe and comforted, and so I promise you this. You will never know a moment's peace. Your life with me will be an agony. I will make you an addict for my touch, my gaze, the barest possibility of my approval. You will live for it. And you will never be happy. You will never feel safe. You will be nothing more than a junkie. Strung out on a man who will never love you back. Ever."

Then he took her hand in his, a parody of the kind of touch a bride might expect on the first day of her marriage. And he led her from the boat, onto that hateful rock, where the brooding old castle rose into the sky.

But Josselyn knew that her doom was not in those weathered rocks, rich with history and pain. It walked beside her, made of flesh and spite.

Because her tragedy was that despite everything he had said and done since he'd found her waiting for him on the plane, she already wanted him.

Meaning he had already won.

# CHAPTER FOUR

BUT SHE DID not have to make it easy for him.

Josselyn jerked her hand away from Cenzo's once she was off the boat. She charged ahead of him along the jetty toward the narrow, endless stairs that climbed up from the rocky beach. And instead of standing about, politely offering to lend a hand as they began unloading the luggage so she could settle into her imprisonment in style, she did what she'd been wanting to do for what seemed like a lifetime now.

She ran. Up the stairs and away from the boat. Away from *him*.

His words seemed to chase her, blaring within her and snarling like demons at her heels.

The stairs wound around and around the outside of the castle, and she ordered herself to slow down when her breath deserted her. Before her heart clawed its way out. The climb was steep and his words only seemed to echo more loudly inside her, but as she slowed she noticed something else. This might be a rocky ruin of an island, but the view was stunning.

The Mediterranean Sea stretched out in all directions, an impossible blue. Josselyn assumed the land she saw in the distance, not quite over the horizon, was Sicily. The morning was bright and though the breeze was cool, it felt as if it might warm as the day went on. If she'd found this place on a vacation of some kind, she thought she might have found it charming.

And what struck her then, as she accepted the beauty of even so desolate a place, was the quiet.

She couldn't think when she'd last been so utterly by herself. If she ignored the evil bridegroom issue—as she felt she needed to do or she would simply scream and leap from the stairs to dash herself on the rocks below, something that felt unduly dramatic—she could hear the sound of high-above birds. Waves below as they surged against the rocks. The breeze rushing through the very few trees and down from the heights.

It was stark and it was lonely, but that didn't make it any less beautiful.

Josselyn told herself she would hold on to that. Somehow.

And on she climbed.

The ruined part of the castle intrigued her, but she somehow doubted that the richest man alive planned to camp there, exposed to the elements, no matter what lesson he thought that might teach *her*. She passed the half-fallen walls and the stairs began to widen, eventually leading her up from the rubble to a kind of landing and an old stone gate.

She pushed her way through it and stopped short.

Because she'd expected nothing but stark ruins and crumbling stone, but the moment Josselyn stepped through the gate, she could see that this castle was not nearly as abandoned as it looked from below. Not the highest part of it. She now stood in the forecourt of a small keep, but on this side of the gate everything was…polished. It *gleamed*. She crossed over the stones, her boot heels beating out a cadence as she moved. And when she reached the other side, the great wooden doors that greeted her opened soundlessly and easily.

Inside, she found the same old stone walls but with new windows to let in the light. In the place of the dreary antiques or possibly prison cells she'd anticipated, she found open spaces, hints of modern steel, every furnishing clearly carefully chosen to make everything seem bright and new.

She was still trying to take that in when she heard the door open behind her, and whirled around to face Cenzo once again.

Her heart, having settled down, leaped into high gear again.

"I told you that you would not be harmed," Cenzo

said. "I see that you did not entirely believe me. Perhaps you even wished that you might end up in the dungeons, all the better to martyr yourself."

"As a matter fact, I'm not a martyr at all."

"Are you not?"

He prowled inside, and suddenly the great hall that had felt airy and light to her moments before seemed to close in on top of her. It had something to do with the way he trained those hawk's eyes upon her, as if he was only waiting for the right moment to swoop in and eat her whole.

Her heart kicked at her and her belly twisted at that notion, but between her legs she was shamefully hot.

"I'm really not," she told him. "I didn't do as my father asked because it brought me some pleasure to sacrifice myself to his desires. Or to yours. I did it because I love him. And I understand him. I like that I can take care of him in this way after the lifetime he spent caring for me."

His smile was a mirthless blade. "You might as well not bother trying to convince me that your father is a good man, Josselyn. I know better."

"And will you tell me what sins my father committed against yours?" she demanded, taking a kind of refuge in the temper that kicked in her then. It was far better than the other, more worrying things she felt. Like attraction. Or the competing sense that she should not go about bringing up his lost father—and no matter that he seemed to have no qualm using that loss as a weapon. She knew that *she* would not react well if he threw her mother at her in this way. She hated that she felt shaky, deep inside, as she pushed on. "Surely if the crime requires this kind of punishment, I should at least know the details."

"In time, *cara*," Cenzo murmured, those eyes of his gleaming. "In time."

His men entered the hall then and did not pause in the great hall, seemingly knowing already precisely where they needed to go. Josselyn had the sudden notion that if she went now and ran full out, she could race down the stairs, take the boat, and leave them all here to rot.

But Cenzo only laughed, dark and low.

"You can try," he told her, as if he'd read her mind that easily. "But I will catch you before you make it to the gate. And I do not think you will appreciate my response."

Her lips tingled at that, reliving the crush of his hard mouth to hers. She told herself she'd hated it, but it still took everything she had to keep from lifting her fingers to touch her lips, to see if they still felt like hers after he'd imprinted himself upon her.

The trouble was, she believed him. She believed that he would chase her and catch her, and more than that, she understood what he hadn't said. That it was not so much what he might do—but the simple fact that running like that would encourage him to put his hands on her body.

Josselyn might have been innocent, an accident that had somehow gone on for more years than she would have thought possible when it had never been a *plan* of hers or any kind of statement, but that didn't make her an idiot. Whatever she might want to call what happened when they touched, it was clearly combustible.

And given what he told her he intended to do with her, it was obviously in her best interest that she see to it they touched as little as possible.

She turned away from him then—away from her escape route—and followed his men. Or rather, the men carrying her luggage, hoping that at some point they would veer off from the others and settle her somewhere far away from their master.

But no such luck. She had a brief tour of lovely rooms clearly modernized with an eye toward bringing the sea and the sky inside, then she was led up into a high tower. Where all the men with all the luggage climbed all the winding stairs to the top until they reached the sprawling master suite.

And, naturally, Cenzo was standing there in the doorway when all the men retreated.

Blocking her exit, if she wasn't mistaken. Again.

"You can't really think that we're going to share a room, can you?" Josselyn crossed her arms, but mostly because she wanted to make sure that if she started shaking, he couldn't see it. "Do you actually imagine that there's any possibility we're just going to leap into bed together?"

"I would not be averse to it." He looked amused when she scowled. "But there are no other bedrooms here, I am afraid. I told you. The *castello* is a place for solitary reflection. There is only the one bed."

"Then I am very sorry that you will have to sleep on the hard stone floor somewhere," she said, with an admirable stab at a sweet tone. "I know you seem to think that I'll be writhing about on the floor in the throes of a sex addiction soon enough, but I'm happy to say that no such addiction currently exists. So if you'll excuse me, I need to freshen up after an overnight flight and a round of unwanted kisses and unhinged threats from my brand-new husband."

Josselyn expected him to argue, but instead, all he did was laugh again. That damnable laugh of his that made her shudder, then overheat. He sketched a deeply mocking bow, there in the doorway. And she couldn't believe it when he…turned and left. She actually ran to the door herself to make sure that he really was walking down the stone stairs, leaving only the sound of his footsteps behind as he went round the bend at each landing.

Was she happy he'd left her? Or did she feel something…more complicated?

She opted not to analyze that too closely. The first thing she did was go back into the sprawling bedchamber and close the door behind her, not particularly surprised to find it had no lock. Then she pulled out her phone and checked to see if what he'd said was true. Sure enough, there was no cell phone service. No Wi-Fi. Though all around her the Mediterranean lolled about seductively on the other side of the windows, she found the quiet seemed a little more ominous, suddenly.

And the curses she muttered under her breath, then not so under her breath, didn't help any.

Still, Josselyn did what she could. She checked to see that the bathroom did, in fact, have a lock—and that was the only reason she drew herself a bath, then settled into it, trying to soak her equilibrium back.

And it worked well enough, because she was certainly calmer when she got out. She supposed that if she was to be locked away here for a month, it was a nice touch that the bath was fully outfitted, like a spa, so she could while away her terrible honeymoon with luxurious bath salts and a view.

Josselyn meant to march back downstairs the moment she was dressed, to confront Cenzo yet again, but instead she found herself drawn to a cozy chair that sat in one of the tower's sunny alcoves, offering her nothing but the sea and the sky. She curled up there, intending to gaze out for only a moment or so, but instead, nodded off to sleep.

And when she woke again, with a start, she could tell from the light outside that hours had passed.

Maybe it was a good thing. Maybe she could spend this month catching up on her sleep—because Lord knew, she had been plagued with sleepless nights ever since Cenzo Falcone had turned up in the family cottage in Maine that day.

She splashed cold water on her face, avoided her reflection in the glass, and then set off to see what, exactly, she was dealing with.

Josselyn told herself she was exploring, that was all. And that was what she did. First to see if what he'd told her was true. And she found that though there were other doors in the tower, they led to rooms…but not to other bedchambers. There was a small library. A sitting room. Something that she would have considered a yoga room if it had belonged to anyone else.

But no other bedrooms. And not even a sofa big enough to act like a bed in a pinch.

Down in the main part of the new castle, she accepted that she was looking for her husband only when she made no effort at all to run toward the door now that no one was guarding it.

Was he right, after all? Was this how it started? Was she to be drawn to him against her very will?

"Don't be ridiculous," she told herself sternly. "You're trying to salvage something from this situation, that's all. It's perfectly rational."

But she didn't feel particularly rational when she found him in the large kitchen. His intensity seemed to her like a living thing. Like a hand that reached out and caught her up, then held her in a fist.

Cenzo stood at a center island surrounded by steel and inviting tile, a rack of copper pans hanging above him, while he wielded what looked like a very, very sharp knife. She could see the old hearth on one side and could imagine that it had once been the center of the castle, but today it stood cold. And Cenzo appeared to be preparing food, which struck her as… Well, as nothing short of astonishing.

"I trust you slept well," he said, without looking up. In a mild tone that very nearly sounded friendly.

Something skittered around inside her at the idea that he'd looked in on her while she slept. She wanted it to be dismay, and she told herself it was, but it was too warm for that. Much too warm.

"I find it difficult to believe that you actually know how to cook," Josselyn said, maybe too severely. She tried to breathe through her *dismay*. "Surely in all your other many residences, you are besieged by servants ready and eager to meet your every need before it forms."

"I am." He was chopping up tomatoes and tossing them in a small pot before him. "But there are a few places I go where it is only me. And if I would like it to remain only me, that means I must take care of my own needs. The first time I attempted it,

I cannot say the cooking was a success. So I hired a chef to teach me. Because it turns out that even on my own, I insist upon a certain standard."

Josselyn found herself clinging to the kitchen door. "Why are you telling me anecdotes about yourself?" She swallowed, not surprised to find her throat was dry. "Are you trying to lure me in with a false sense of camaraderie?"

Those predator's eyes met hers. "Yes."

She huffed out a breath. "Well. Points for honesty, I guess."

"I am not, as you have said, a liar, Josselyn. I did not lie to your father. I merely did not correct him. These are not the same thing."

She drifted farther into the kitchen, feeling not unlike Persephone creeping into the underworld. Because there was a platter before him with what looked like cheese and bread, and her stomach rumbled. But she dared not take any. Wasn't that the rule? Eat something and you were doomed to stay in hell forever.

On the other hand, she was really hungry.

It helped that Cenzo did not appear to care overmuch what she did. He carried on fixing the meal before him, as if he was alone in the renovated kitchen. Josselyn crept closer and decided it would do her no good to ignore the physical realities of a situation.

*You really do need your strength*, she told herself piously.

And though she could feel Cenzo's gaze on her from time to time as she stood across from him, every time she glanced at him he appeared to be entirely engrossed in preparing a pasta dish.

Long before she was anywhere near satiated, he whisked the cheese and bread away. He carried the platter out through doors she'd thought were windows, leading her out to a wide terrace off the side of the kitchen. It seemed to hang there over the sea, nothing but the horizon in the distance and exultant bougainvillea closer in, clinging to the rail.

"Sit," he ordered her.

And he did not wait to see if she would obey; he simply strode off back into the kitchen.

To say that she had whiplash would be vastly understating the situation. Josselyn moved to the bright and fragrant rail, because despite the careening sort of feeling inside her, she couldn't keep herself from staring out at the sea. She didn't *want* to keep herself from it. The Mediterranean was deep blue and beckoning, and the ruckus inside her shifted into a kind of thrill. It was as if she couldn't tell what her body might do of its own accord, suddenly. It felt entirely possible that she might simply find herself leaping off the terrace. Hurling herself out into all that glorious blue.

And not because she was filled with the need to

end herself. But because she thought that for a while there, she might actually fly.

She heard a sound behind her and turned to find Cenzo coming toward her again, this time bearing two plates of the pasta he'd made. And she couldn't help but notice that looking at him felt very much the same as looking down from this great height to the sea far below.

He set out the plates on the table, which was perfectly placed to take in the view, and took one of the seats. Then did nothing, save raise one brow.

And wait.

Josselyn didn't move. "I'm trying to fit in a homemade dinner with the list of threats you unspooled for me earlier. I didn't expect to be enslaved via food."

"It is the way to the heart, Josselyn. Surely you have heard this, even in the rustic wilds of your Pennsylvania."

It was a bit rich to call Pennsylvania rustic and wild when they were currently perched on the top of a big rock, with civilization far off beyond the horizon. And yet she drifted toward the table despite herself.

She told herself it was the pasta. "I think you're going to have to explain to me how and why you're pursuing this remarkably intimate bid for my destruction. Surely you could also put me under house arrest in one of your many properties and leave me to rot."

"But that would not give me what I want." Cenzo indicated the empty seat opposite him with a peremptory hand.

Josselyn should have ignored it. She should have made a stand, started how she meant to go on, and made it clear he couldn't treat her like this. But again, she was hungry and she doubted very much that he would stoop to poisoning her. And in any case, even if it was poisoned, and/or it kept her in his underworld forever, it smelled delicious.

She took her seat, glad that she'd kept her sweater on though the day looked sunny and warm. Maybe it was, but here up high where the castle pierced the sky, the sea breeze was constant.

"*Mangia,*" Cenzo murmured, and then they each set to the task of eating.

And Josselyn was far too aware, of everything. Every possible sensation. She felt the wind play with her hair and toy with what little skin was exposed. She felt the sun, pleasingly warm but never hot, and far off she could hear the seabirds sharing songs with each other as they flew.

"This is delicious," she said. She couldn't help herself.

"It is Pasta alla Norma," he replied. "It is Catanian." His gaze swept to hers, then lowered. "That is, from farther down the coast."

The food he'd prepared was simple. Sicilian, apparently. And the flavors burst on her tongue, making her feel something like seduced.

Then again, maybe Josselyn was kidding herself. Maybe it had nothing to do with the food or the sea air or her admittedly scenic location. Maybe what she was truly aware of here was the man.

Cenzo had changed his clothing while she slept— and she didn't want to think about him doing such a thing in the same room where she'd slumbered on, unaware. It made her breath catch. Now he wore more casual dark trousers and a T-shirt that looked as if it might, very possibly, have been created specifically to glorify his form. He should have looked less dangerous out of the bespoke suits that she'd thought he lived in. But instead, the change did the opposite.

It had nothing to do with the clothes. There was no disguising that the brooding, elemental danger that exuded from him was as much a part of him as that old coin profile. His predator's gaze. That cruel mouth that made her hunger for another taste—

What she couldn't understand, she thought as she very carefully placed her utensils back on her plate, was how he'd known.

He could not possibly have anticipated that there would be any attraction on her part. Attraction was far too funny. It waxed or waned or failed to turn up at all, based entirely on the individuals involved.

Their history, their needs, and simply how they were wired.

Yet he had sounded so sure that no matter who she might have been, he would have been able to elicit the same response in her.

"You're scowling at me," he pointed out.

"I want to circle back to my heroin addiction, such as it is."

"You might find that you wish for such sweet oblivion, when I'm done with you," he replied. Conversationally, which made it worse. It took a few moments to fully land, and then it seemed to sit on her.

She made herself sit up straighter. "I don't know what makes you think I find you remotely attractive. For all you know, I could be actively working to conceal my repulsion. Like bile in my throat."

Those copper and gold eyes gleamed. "You do not find me repulsive, Josselyn."

"You don't actually know that. I've had a great deal of practice concealing what I actually feel about anything. I'm very good at it."

Cenzo pushed his plate away and sat back in his chair. He looked like a man at ease, but she could feel the weight of his stare. "Let us say that I was in some doubt about your reaction to me, though I am not. It would not matter in any way. We are isolated here. And I will tell you this, *mia moglie.*

I have found that where there is attention, attraction follows."

"You're either attracted to a person or you're not." She shrugged as if it was all out of her hands. "It's not mutable."

"Shall we test it?" He laughed when she shrank back. "I rather thought not."

Josselyn tried to look as if she indeed had bile in her throat instead of too much molten heat charging through her and settling low in her belly. "In case you wondered, I have found your kisses rather lacking. If a man of your much-vaunted prowess and certain narcissism takes notes on his performance."

She had the sense of his laughter, though all he did was smile. "We were speaking in generalities, yes? The mythic possibility that I might encounter a woman who does not want me. I like a fairy story as much as the next person, but let us turn our attention instead to you, Josselyn."

Nothing about the way he was sitting or looking at her changed, yet she still felt as if that noose was around her neck again. And pulling tight.

Only she had never heard of a noose making a person burn like this, all the way through, until she had to fight off the urge to squirm in her seat.

Cenzo considered her for a moment. Maybe three. "You do know that one of the chief inducements your father offered me was your innocence, do you not?"

Josselyn felt her chin rise when what she wanted to do was scream at the violation of her privacy. "You've mentioned my innocence before. I hate to be the one to break this to you, but that ship sailed a long, long time ago."

"Did it?" Cenzo's eyes gleamed. "I think not."

"I couldn't give my virginity away quickly enough," Josselyn declared, lying through her teeth. "You went to boarding school. You must know what it was like. I don't believe any virgins were permitted to graduate from the hallowed halls of my high school."

"Your father seemed certain," Cenzo said. Also sounding certain.

Josselyn nearly laughed, because the absurdity of this conversation was too much. She was sitting in a half-ruined, half-renovated castle somewhere off the coast of Sicily, debating her virginity. Literally discussing it as if it was an estate sale item, like some former doyenne's silver. It was so absurd, in fact, that she couldn't muster up any of the numerous emotional reactions she suspected she was likely to have regarding it—but later. She counted herself lucky for that.

"I don't know how to break this to you," she told him, some of that near-laughter in her voice, "but my father is quite literally the last person on earth with whom I would ever discuss my sex life."

But Cenzo only smiled in that edgy, knowing

way of his. "What I was going to say, *cara*, is that your father was very certain, yes. But I too live in the world. And am well aware that fathers are often the last to know what it is their daughters get up to. Yet any doubts I might have had were completely erased that afternoon in Maine."

Josselyn could still remember it all with such painful clarity. The shock of it, of him. Lounging there against an ancient fireplace, electric and impossible.

"Don't be ridiculous," she said now. "As I believe you've already pointed out, we didn't even speak."

"Words were unnecessary." He gave the impression of shrugging without quite doing so, though his gaze was even more intent. "Your eyes grew big. You stopped breathing. Then you turned red. Not, I think, the typical behavior of an experienced woman."

Josselyn had never felt her virginity like any kind of burden. She'd retained it through chance, not deliberation. It was difficult to have any kind of a social life when she spent most of her time in her father's company. And during her college years— and indeed throughout boarding school—when she'd been left to her own devices, she'd never really managed to understand how a person got from one place to the other. The flinging off of clothes had never seemed organic to her. Did one person start and the other follow? Did both parties agree to undress and then proceed from there in a kind of lockstep? It had always seemed fraught with tension and potential mishaps, so she couldn't even say that she'd avoided it. It was more the opportunity had never arisen.

She now wished that she'd spent more time applying herself to the issue.

But she only sniffed at Cenzo. "It's too bad that your Ivy League education failed to make it clear to you that a person's virginity is not, in fact, visible when they walk into a room."

"Generally speaking, no," he agreed. "But yours is."

That was horrifying to contemplate. "I'm not going to argue with you, Cenzo. It's pointless. Of the two people sitting here, I'm the only one who actually knows my sexual history."

A normal person might have looked abashed at that. But this was Cenzo Falcone. All he ever seemed to look was amused.

Josselyn forged on. "What I'd like to know is how, if you truly believe that I remained virginal all this time, you think that you can simply swan in and not only get me into bed but make me a slavering addict where you're concerned. You don't suffer from insecurity, do you?"

"I am a man who was taught since birth to know his consequence." Cenzo waved a hand. "My worth is not a mere concept to me, to be trotted out in sad self-help seminars. I know it to the decimal."

"I see. You intend to treat me like a bank balance. And that, you seem so confident, will render me so enslaved to you that it will break my father's heart from afar." Josselyn sat back in her chair and tried to look as unconcerned as he did. "This seems a bit far-fetched, I have to say."

"That is because you do not understand," he said, almost sounding warm. Inviting. If they had been discussing any other topic, she was sure she would have been confused. She would have imagined that somehow, this was nothing more than a domestic moment between a husband and wife.

Was that what he wanted her to think? Was it just another example of his mind games?

"I have studied your family," Cenzo told her, with perhaps too much portent in his words for her liking. "You were very young when your mother and brother died."

"I was ten." And it was funny how grief changed over time. She didn't feel the sharp edge of it any longer. She wouldn't like it if someone wielded it as a weapon, in temper, but she didn't mind when people brought up her family tragedy of their own volition. Because it was a simple fact that happened to be her personal history. Her mother and older brother had sailed out into Blue Hill Bay that summer's day and had never returned.

Nothing ever made that better. But then again, it wasn't as if anything could make it worse.

"There were those who expected your father to remarry, especially with a young daughter yet to raise. But he did not. He raised you himself, and as far as anyone is aware, never had the slightest interest in another woman."

"Their marriage was arranged, much as ours was," Josselyn said, nodding. "But the difference is, they quickly fell in love. I think my father has always felt that there is no possibility that he could ever hope that lightning might strike twice for him."

"How romantic." Cenzo did not sneer, but he certainly made it clear that he did not find that story romantic at all. "It has been nearly twenty years. It is clear to even the most casual observer that if your father is capable of loving anything at all, he loves you."

She laughed, more in shock than because she thought that was funny. "If he's capable? Let me assure you, he is. Of course he loves me. As I love him in return."

"So tender," Cenzo murmured, and this time, the sardonic inflection seemed to leave marks in her flesh. "But you see, that is exactly what I will use."

It shouldn't have felt like whiplash. She'd known he was playing games here. Still, she found herself winded once more.

And worse, molten hot straight through. Because apparently being more or less kidnapped and marooned on an island was the key to making her think about taking off her clothes. Who could have guessed?

"You speak so much of how you will use me," she managed to say. "Enslave me. Addict me. A lot of implied action and danger, I'd say. But when given the opportunity to show me how intimidated I should be by all your bluster, all you did was cook pasta and slice up some cheese."

"It's only the first day," Cenzo said, and smiled as if he was approachable. Or as if he wanted her to *think* he was approachable...if only for a moment. "But I want to be clear about the aim here. Your father is used to your attention. To being the center of your world. You think he is capable of love. I do not."

"Oh," she said mildly, "look at that. Another topic that I know more about than you."

He ignored her, lounging there as if daring the Sicilian sun to render itself prostrate before him too. "Either way, Josselyn, when I take all that you have to give he will be left with nothing. And you will be too far gone to care."

# CHAPTER FIVE

CENZO WAS ENJOYING HIMSELF.

Truly, this had all gone better than he could have imagined, and he had spent the past two years imagining it in every possible permutation. What she might say, what she might do. Having studied her extensively, he thought he'd been prepared.

But Josselyn defied study. And he hadn't been prepared for his response to her. He certainly couldn't have known that a simple conversation with this wife he had not wanted eclipsed any other form of entertainment in his memory.

He told himself that boded well for his plans and nothing more. For she was the quarry, not he.

*And yet you seem to need reminders*, a voice in him, sounding far too much like Françoise, commented acidly.

"I don't understand," Josselyn said, though he thought she lied. Her color was high again, though he would not share that with her. Not when it seemed such an excellent barometer of her reactions. Her dark eyes were glossy, her mouth militant. She stayed where she was, sitting perhaps too still after having eaten a meal he'd prepared with his own hands. He had intended to throw her off-balance. What he had not prepared for was how deeply such a thing would affect him in turn.

Because it turned out that he liked it. He liked that his wife should eat what he had made. He liked watching her eat. He liked talking to her, because he never knew what she might say when so many of the people he interacted with bored him silly. He liked too much of this—of her—particularly when it felt like the kind of intimacy he did not intend to allow.

But he assured himself that as time passed here, the effect these things would have on her would far outstrip any reaction of his own.

"Do you truly not understand?" he asked her. "Or is it that you imagine you can somehow appeal to my better angels if you pretend that you do not? Let me save you the trouble. I have none."

If he expected her to wilt, he was in for disappointment. If anything, she sat straighter, managing to look somehow regal. He supposed it was another form of armor.

Cenzo intended to strip it away. Every bit of it.

"I'm not attempting to make any kind of appeal," she said, sounding cool and unbothered. But he could see the way her eyes flashed and knew better. "All I'm trying to do is figure out what it is you believe will occur between us over the next month. I don't need an agenda, but I am interested in the specifics. So far, all of it is very vague. It will all be terrible. I will be ruined. My father will be torn asunder, blah blah blah."

"I like this," Cenzo said, amused. "Show me your fangs, little one. They are adorable."

She stood up then, abruptly. He thought she might storm off into the castle, but as ever, she surprised him. Josselyn moved instead to the rail, gripped it, and stared out toward the sea.

"If you're thinking of jumping," he said with great indolence, "I would advise against it. It's not a straight shot, you see. You would likely live, in some or other reduced capacity. Not quite the dramatic gesture I imagine you're going for."

"I have no intention of jumping."

She turned back, and he had the interesting notion that this was perhaps the first time they had truly gazed at each other. No artifice, no shock. No manners.

And unsmiling, she was actually even more beautiful. There was nothing to take away from the simple, stunning architecture of her face. And that beauty mark that directed attention straight to that mouth of hers. He intended to taste her and take his time with it.

Soon.

Because of his plan, he assured himself. All of this was in service to the plan.

"There is no agenda," he told her, eventually, when she was beginning to look agitated. "I assume you have studied up on me, as I have you." He did not wait for her to confirm it. And besides, he was Cenzo Falcone. There was only so much study required. "Then you know that when I set myself to a task, I achieve it."

"I was under the impression that wasn't an issue of character, in your case," she said, her tone as even as her gaze was dark. "So much as unlimited funds to back any decision you might choose to make."

"Does it make a difference? I have spent the past two years studying your weaknesses so that I might use them against you. Your devotion to your father, check. Your martyr complex, check."

"If I had a martyr complex," she retorted, "I would be halfway into a swan dive even now."

"That is not how a martyr complex works, I think. It's the heat of the pyre that matters and the audience to behold it, not the actual immolation. But it is of no matter. Now that it is only the two of us, stranded here for weeks, there will be nothing to do all day, every day, but find buttons. And then push them."

"I admire your confidence that you will be the one pushing those buttons," she said softly. "As if I will be doing nothing at all but sitting idly by, waiting to see what you might use against me next."

"But you see, I cannot be pushed," he told her, almost apologetically. When inside, the dragon in him shot fire. "At the end of the day, *cara*, there is someone you will wish to protect. That leaves you weak. I have no such weaknesses."

"You do not wish to protect your own mother?"

"Françoise Falcone requires no protection," Cenzo assured her. "And even if she did, there is no possibility that you could ever leverage her against me. For whatever I might think of your family, her opinion is worse. Much worse."

Josselyn frowned. "Is that why she didn't attend the wedding?"

"She understands why I am doing this but felt she could not accord it her blessing." He inclined his head in a gesture that he knew looked like contrition on others. Not so much on him. "You understand."

"How odd." Josselyn let out a half-laugh. "My father thought it was because she was embarrassed."

The very idea had him laughing out loud. A real laugh, even.

"I have seen my mother in many moods, but I have never seen her embarrassed." He shook his head. "Though it is true that she feels that any American, by virtue of the newness and greenness of your connections, must be beneath not only the Falcone line but her own family, who trace their blood to the House of Bourbon."

"You misunderstand me," Josselyn said, a curious expression on her face. It made him wonder if he'd misjudged her—but no. That was impossible. Cenzo did not make mistakes. "I don't think bloodlines have anything to do with it. My father assumed your mother did not wish to show her face after she'd made such a play for him. And was, of course, denied."

"I beg your pardon?"

His wife did not seem to recognize her danger. She was leaning back against the rail now, suddenly looking entirely at her ease. A whisper of something washed over him, though he did not immediately recognize what it was.

It took him another moment to realize that it was apprehension.

But surely that was not possible either. He held all the cards in this. She had never been anything but a lamb to the slaughter.

And more, she thought the man he knew was to blame for the grief in him that never dissipated was *good*.

He held on to that outrage.

"I was only ten when my mother died, as you've already established," Josselyn said, sounding easier with every syllable. "My father used to tell me stories at bedtime, and he didn't read to me from books. He told me stories about my mother and my brother. About how funny and bright and brave Jack was, and how now he could act as my big brother no matter where I was. And about how he and my mother met, and fell in love, and built a life together. This became our tradition."

There was absolutely no reason, Cenzo assured himself, that he should feel a trickle of foreboding move down the back of his neck.

She was still speaking. "When I outgrew needing to be tucked into bed, every night we were together my father would still tell me stories about the past. I think it helped him as much as me, if I'm honest. And one of the stories he liked to tell was how he thought that perhaps he had fallen in love with my mother from afar. For how else could he explain that when his engagement was announced, a woman who he considered his best friend's, who he had always admired, propositioned him. But he turned her down for a woman he hardly knew."

Cenzo felt everything in him still. "Your father is a liar. Better you should know it now and stop spreading his poison."

Josselyn looked unmoved. "I don't think your parents had been married long. They all knew each other well, didn't they? The stories Papa tells of their youth seem like something out of a Hemingway book. A movable feast with the three of them all over Europe, your mother the woman that half the men they knew were in love with."

"My mother would no more lower herself to an American—" Cenzo began in a fury.

"Well, you're quite right, but only because my father didn't accept her offer."

"I feel certain that my mother is, even now, somehow aware of this slander and has suddenly come over horrified in her villa in Taormina." Cenzo shook his head. "Wherever could you have come by such a notion?"

"She wrote him letters, Cenzo," Josselyn said softly. "So even if I was tempted to think that my father had forgotten what actually happened, or had embellished it, I'm afraid there are the letters to tell a different story."

"You are wrong." Cenzo's voice was flat. "You have obviously never met my mother, for if you did you would know that she is not romantic. She comes from an ancient French line and was raised to concern herself only with how best she could carry forth that legacy."

And more, she had been devoted to his father. She was still devoted to his father.

"If you say so." This wife he'd been so sure he could crush beneath his shoe with little effort gazed back at him as if she knew she'd set off a seismic reaction inside him. She even shrugged as if this was all nothing to her. "But also, for a time, it seems that she was willing to throw it all away for an upstart American all the same."

Cenzo found himself standing and had no idea when he'd decided to move. Temper and something else flooded through him, making him feel a heady mix of lit up and darkly intense, and all of it was focused on the slender woman who stood before him, the Sicilian sun in her hair and the Sicilian Sky on her finger.

And while he watched, she slowly smiled at him.

"Tell me again how it is that you have no buttons to push." She dared him. *She* dared *him*. "And I will tell you more stories about your mother, because believe me, there are many. After our engagement, I went through all my father's correspondence. It was fascinating. Illuminating, even."

Cenzo slashed his hand through the air. And though everything in him urged him to move forward—to put his hands on her, to handle this with his mouth on hers, his hands all over her skin—he held himself back.

Because he hadn't expected this, and that was a problem. He hadn't anticipated that she would turn the tables on him—it hadn't crossed his mind that she *could*—and that would take some thought. Some different plans, perhaps.

Some getting used to, certainly.

And he could not allow himself to lose, in the heat of the moment, what had taken him years of fury and focus to put into motion.

"I see you are a liar much like your own father," he gritted out. "How proud he must be."

But the meek, obedient virgin he had expected to easily break apart only smiled wider.

"That's a nice try," Josselyn said. "But the difference is, I know my father. I know him well. I haven't set him up on any kind of pedestal, and, in fact, have been his employee as well as his daughter, so I can truly say I know more than one side of him. Trust me when I tell you that I am deeply conversant on my father's flaws. He is not a liar. Neither am I." She studied him, still smiling. "But I'm beginning to suspect that your mother is."

Cenzo felt a seething kind of rage build inside him, and the hint of that deep, wild grief behind it, and it was not contained to the usual places. Here, with her, it pooled in his sex and made his skin feel two sizes too small, stretched over his bones.

"I will admit that you surprised me, Josselyn," he managed to say as if he was in full command of himself, as he should have been. "I did not expect you to traffic in such falsehoods. But do not worry. It will change nothing. I simply know better, now, who you really are."

He picked up the plates from the table, taking them, and himself, back inside.

And he was all too aware that she followed him, maneuvering herself so that she once more stood on the other side of the wide, long kitchen island and regarded him in that same steady way.

As if she thought she was in control of this.

"I wouldn't want you to get the wrong impression," she told him, and she was no longer smiling at him, all sharp challenge. "Papa was flattered by your mother's interest in him. The story wasn't told at your mother's expense, ever. He thought too highly of her. It was to highlight that even then, when he could have had a woman who he had long considered the finest of them all, he stuck with my mother instead. When he barely knew her. And before, in fact, they had gone ahead and fallen for each other. You can take that as an insult if you must. But it doesn't come from my father."

"You asked for an agenda." For the first time, possibly ever, Cenzo was not sure that he could keep his voice steady. Until he managed it, somehow. "For today, I suggest you acquaint yourself with this island. Explore it at will. Learn its nooks and crannies, take note of the ruins and the cliffs, and better still, note that there is nowhere to go. The quicker you accept that, the better."

"That was almost a lovely invitation. And then you ruined it."

"I will expect you to dine with me in the evenings," he continued in the same stern way, as if she hadn't spoken. "If you do not present yourself, I will come find you. You will not like that."

"More threats, naturally," she said, almost sunnily. "I see you've recovered from the shock of hearing that your mother is a person, as complicated as anyone else."

Cenzo refused to spend one single moment dignifying her lies—not even with a stray thought about his mother or his parents' often chilly, remote marriage. Not one.

He would blame her father for that, too.

"I intend to sleep in our bed every night," he told her in the same implacable way. "I will not force you to do the same, but you will have noticed, I think, that I meant it when I said there were no other beds here. I would not encourage you to come up with a makeshift one, either. I will not allow it. You may sleep in the marital bed next to your husband, or you may be uncomfortable. The choice is yours."

"You are all heart."

"It is my intention, *cara*, to take the virginity we both know you still possess. And soon. But do not worry unduly. I will not force myself upon you."

"What is an *undue* amount of worry in this situation, Cenzo?"

He only gazed back at her and did nothing to hide the ruthlessness in him. The power of his will. Or his certainty that she would not only bend, but crumble.

"Let me guess," Josselyn said after a moment. "You believe that I will beg you for the pleasure."

"I know you will."

He felt like himself again as she stood there before him, clearly trembling in some kind of outrage, though she fought to conceal it. But he could see it all over her, making her attempt to stand there—straight and tall and drenched in serenity—fall slightly flat.

And he knew she wouldn't believe it, but he could still see her innocence all over her. He could read her too clearly. Her color was heightened once again. Her dark eyes were faintly glassy. And Cenzo had no doubt that if he were to reach over and touch her, her skin would be hot.

Just as he knew that if he reached between her legs, she would be wet.

But these were all discoveries he would force her to make. And then he would use them against her, one after the next.

"I tried to tell you this before," she said, enunciating her words in a manner that he supposed was meant to cut him to ribbons. "But I find you repulsive. Horrific. The only thing I will ever beg you for is a divorce."

She turned at that and marched herself out of the kitchen.

And really, he should have let her go. This was only the first day of a long siege.

But the dragon in him had woken again, and it liked the scent of her. His sex was thick and heavy, and he hungered for a real taste of that mouth of hers. Particularly now that he'd discovered that she truly did have fangs, and more, could use them.

He wanted her naked. He wanted her beneath

him, astride him, on her hands and knees before him, the better to take his thrusts.

And all of these things would be his, he knew. All he need do was wait. And play this game he could already tell he would win. And handsomely.

But first, there was today, and he didn't like the fact that she thought she had the upper hand.

Without questioning himself, Cenzo followed her from the kitchen. He heard her boots against the flagstones, then each step as she started up the stairs into the tower. More, he could hear her temper in every crash of her feet against the old stones.

It was easy enough to catch her, then whirl her around, there in the narrow stairwell.

"But you said—" she began, her eyes wide as she gazed up at him. "You promised—"

"I wish only to kiss my wife," Cenzo growled. "On this, the first day of the rest of our life together."

"You don't want to kiss me," she threw at him, and he thought the way she trembled now was her temper taking hold. The most convenient of the passions, but he would take any. "You want to make one of your grim little points. You want to start what you think will be my downward spiral, until all I can do is fling myself prostrate before you and cringe about at your feet. Guess what? I would rather die."

"Let us test that theory," he suggested, and kissed her.

And this time, it had nothing at all to do with punishment. Though it was no less a claiming.

This time, it was a seduction.

Pleasure and dark promise.

He took her face in his hands, and he tasted her as he wanted at last. He teased her lips until she sighed, melting against him, and opened to let him in.

Then he angled his head and set them both on fire.

He kissed her and he kissed her, until all that fury, all that need, hummed there between them. He kissed her, losing himself in the sheer wonder of her taste and the way that sweet sea scent of hers teased at him, as if she was bewitching him despite his best efforts to seize control.

Cenzo kissed her like a man drowning and she met each thrust of his tongue, then moved closer as if she was as greedy as he was.

As if she knew how much he wanted her and wanted him, too, with that very same intensity.

And there were so many things he wanted to do with her. But kissing her felt like a gift, like sheer magic, and for once in his life, Cenzo lost track of his own ulterior motives. His own grand plan.

There was only her taste. Her heat.

Her hair that he gripped in his hands, and the way she pressed against him.

There was only Josselyn. His wife.

He kissed her again and again, and then he shifted, meaning to lift her in his arms—

But she pushed away from him, enough to brace herself against his chest. He found his hands on her upper arms.

"I agreed to marry you," she managed to pant out at him, her lips faintly swollen and her brown eyes wild. "Not to take part in whatever sick revenge fantasy this is. I refuse to be a pawn in your game."

"You can be any piece on the board that you like," he replied, trying to gather himself. "But it will still be my board, Josselyn."

And he watched something wash over her, intense and deep, and realized that he was holding on to her as if he wished to keep her with him—even if she did not want to stay.

Which defeated the purpose of all of this, didn't it?

And more, made him the monster her father was.

He let her go, lifting up his hands theatrically. "By all means, little wife. Run and hide if that makes you feel more powerful."

And he really thought, in that moment, that Josselyn might take a swing at him. He had no doubt that if she did, the blow would land. It might even sting a little.

He kept his hands in the air, his mock surrender, and laughed at her as he stepped back.

Because he'd forgotten, entirely, that they stood on those narrow stairs.

She had kissed him silly.

It was his own mocking laughter that stayed with him as he fell, a seeming slow-motion slide backward when his foot encountered only air. He saw her face as the world fell out from beneath him.

Nothing but her lovely face.

And then there was nothing.

# CHAPTER SIX

JOSSELYN WATCHED HIM FALL, everything in her seeming to fall with him. Her stomach plummeted to her feet. She flung out her arms as if she could catch him, but missed, doing nothing but rapping her knuckles against the wall.

He twisted in the air, then hit the floor of the next landing with his arms thrust out in front of him, before finally coming to a stop with a sickening thud.

Then he was still.

And this was Cenzo Falcone, so she expected him to leap to his feet again. To rise as if it had been nothing but a trick, so he could laugh at her mockingly all the more. So he could kiss her the way he'd just done, all that wildfire and shocking heat, and make her forget her name all over again—

But though she gripped the stone wall beside her, her eyes fixed on him as he lay there, he did not move.

The only sound was her own heartbeat, a mad

racket in her ears, her breath sawing in and out of her as one horrible moment bled into another.

Josselyn threw herself forward, scrabbling down the stairs and dropping to her knees beside him on the lower landing. What if he was dead? What if—?

She couldn't think it.

A sharp pang bloomed in her chest, feeling too much like grief, but she ignored it. She reached out to touch Cenzo, happier than she wanted to admit that he was warm to the touch and that she could see no distressing, unnatural angles. Her fingers were shaking as she pressed them into his neck, but she was instantly relieved to feel his pulse there. Strong and steady.

"Okay," she said out loud, shocked at her own breathlessness, and that sharpness within. "Okay, he's not dead. Good."

But still he didn't move. She tried to think of any first aid dos and don'ts she might have picked up on over the years. He had fallen backward, but he'd twisted himself around and had somehow landed on his side. As she stared at him, wishing she'd done something useful with her life so she could handle this well, she could see a large, red bruise forming on his forehead.

She didn't think he'd suffered a spinal injury, but a head injury probably wasn't much better.

Josselyn reached for her phone, then stopped in the act of pulling it from her back pocket, swearing under her breath as she remembered. No cell phone service. No Wi-Fi. No possible means of contacting the outside world. She remembered that he'd said something about a radio. But she had no idea where one might be, or even how she would explain where they were or what had happened.

Could she take the time to look? Did she dare leave him? What if he lapsed off and died while she was scrabbling around the old castle for a radio that, for all she knew, he might have lied about having in the first place?

He murmured something then, his voice sounding thick and unused. She didn't think that he was speaking in English. Or even Italian, for that matter. Josselyn was relieved that he was speaking at all.

And she made a command decision, there and then.

"Come on," she said briskly, trying to put her arm around his back, thinking that might help him figure out how to get to his feet, since she certainly couldn't lift him. "Cenzo. You have to get up."

And to her surprise, he moved. First onto his knees, looking woozy, before pulling himself to his feet. She expected him to blink away the wooziness and then light into her, but he didn't. He only stared at her as if he couldn't place her, and then looked as if he might slump there against the wall and topple on the rest of the stairs.

"We have to move," she told him.

She didn't question that decision as she helped him down the stairs, sometimes shouldering his weight when he faltered, until they reached the main floor of the renovated bit of the castle.

But she didn't stop there, either. Because Cenzo moved with her when she encouraged him, clearly in a daze, and that was how she managed to get him all the way down to that rocky little landing on what passed for the beach. One step at a time, while the Sicilian afternoon grew deep gold and a richer blue around them.

The dinghy looked safer for a man of his size, but she led him toward the small sailboat instead, because there was no way she was going to row across the sea. She thought they were just as likely to end up in Greece when her arms gave out and the current took over.

But one thing Josselyn knew how to do was sail.

She raised the sail and was pleasantly surprised to find it intact. Then she managed to get Cenzo into the boat as she pushed off, still not quite thinking through what it was she was doing. There was no medical attention for him on this island. That had to be the priority. For all she knew, if she hadn't wrestled him down all those stairs, she would still be searching all over the castle for the radio that— best case scenario—he'd probably hidden away to keep her from finding it.

And maybe that was all rationalization so she

wouldn't have to think about things like kissing him until she felt inside out, despite everything he'd said to her this day, much less that grief at the sight of him fallen—but by the time she accepted that she was tacking out of the tiny, rocky cove and heading toward the mainland.

Across from her, Cenzo had slumped down against the gunwale. And no matter how she tried to rouse him with her foot against his leg as well as her voice, he didn't move.

If she wasn't mistaken, he was unconscious.

That couldn't be good.

Josselyn did the only thing she could. She gripped the tiller and kept sailing, letting the wind do the work and hoping that she'd made the right decision.

It had taken her a long time to get Cenzo down those stairs, so she was chasing daylight across the water. As she neared land, she was grateful to see some lights go on ahead of her to show her the way. Because otherwise, who knew where she would have ended up?

She found her way to a tiny harbor and was happy that she could tie the boat up at an actual dock rather than trying to haul it ashore with Cenzo still seemingly unconscious. And then, having done it, she had a moment's worry as she considered her situation. Should she leave him here? Or try to rouse him again and see if she could make him stumble his way toward whatever kind of village this was?

He lay there, slumped against the side of the boat, and even so, there was no mistaking who he was. His power was evident even in repose. But with his eyes closed, it was easier to get lost in the perfectly sculpted lines of his face. To wonder about those stern yet sensual lips of his that she now knew far more intimately—

But there was no time for that, she told herself as the same heat that had overtaken her in that tower stairwell walloped her again. And so inappropriately. The man was hurt, and no matter her feelings about him, she was certainly not going to leave him to die while she dithered about his *lips*.

That thought spurred her into action. She vaulted out of the sailboat onto the dock, then charged her way up into the village. She slipped the Sicilian Sky off her finger as she walked, tucking it into her pocket, and told herself it was only smart not to brandish such a valuable piece of jewelry about in a strange place where she was more or less on her own.

Once in the tiny medieval village, she used her rusty Italian and got directions, not to a hospital, but to the local doctor.

"A retired doctor, *capisci*," said the kindly older man as he and the woman Josselyn had taken for his nurse, but who was likely his wife, rushed with her back down to the docks. "This is a small vil-

# Loyal Readers
# FREE BOOKS Voucher

## We're giving away **THOUSANDS**

**of** **FREE**

**BOOKS**

**Sizzling Romance**

**Passionate Romance**

**Don't Miss Out! Send for Your Free Books Today!**

# Get up to 4 FREE FABULOUS BOOKS You Love!

To thank you for being a loyal reader we'd like to send you up to 4 FREE BOOKS, absolutely free.

Just write "YES" on the Loyal Reader Voucher and we'll send you up to 4 Free Books and Free Mystery Gifts, altogether worth over $20, as a way of saying thank you for being a loyal reader.

Try **Harlequin® Desire** books featuring the worlds of the American elite with juicy plot twists, delicious sensuality and intriguing scandal.

Try **Harlequin Presents®** Larger-print books featuring the glamourous lives of royals and billionaires in a world of exotic locations, where passion knows no bounds.

Or **TRY BOTH!**

We are so glad you love the books as much as we do and can't wait to send you great new books.

So don't miss out, return your Loyal Reader Voucher Today!

*Pam Powers*

# LOYAL READER
# FREE BOOKS VOUCHER

## YES! I Love Reading, please send me up to 4 FREE BOOKS and Free Mystery Gifts from the series I select.

Just write in "YES" on the dotted line below then return this card today and we'll send your free books & gifts asap!

➡️ YES ⬅️
_ _ _ _

Which do you prefer?

☐ **Harlequin Desire®**
225/326 HDL GRGA

☐ **Harlequin Presents® Larger Print**
176/376 HDL GRGA

☐ **BOTH**
225/326 & 176/376
HDL GRGM

| | |
|---|---|
| FIRST NAME | LAST NAME |

ADDRESS

| | |
|---|---|
| APT.# | CITY |

| | |
|---|---|
| STATE/PROV. | ZIP/POSTAL CODE |

EMAIL ☐ Please check this box if you would like to receive newsletters and promotional emails from Harlequin Enterprises ULC and its affiliates. You can unsubscribe anytime.

HD/HP-520-LR21

BUSINESS REPLY MAIL
FIRST-CLASS MAIL    PERMIT NO. 717    BUFFALO, NY

POSTAGE WILL BE PAID BY ADDRESSEE

HARLEQUIN READER SERVICE
PO BOX 1341
BUFFALO NY 14240-8571

NO POSTAGE
NECESSARY
IF MAILED
IN THE
UNITED STATES

▼ If offer card is missing write to: Harlequin Reader Service, P.O. Box 1341, Buffalo, NY 14240-8531 or visit www.ReaderService.com ▼

lage. For a hospital it is necessary to go all the way to Taormina, but here I take care of what I can."

"It's very kind of you," Josselyn managed to pant out as they hurried along.

And it took the three of them, working together, to get Cenzo out of the boat. Then to move him along into the town, and to the doctor's small, makeshift office. Once again, he seemed half-roused but something like drunk as he shambled along, then seemed to pass out when he was lying on the exam table.

"He tripped and fell," Josselyn told the doctor as he checked Cenzo's vitals. The older man frowned as he examined that growing bruise on Cenzo's forehead. "I'm afraid he fell hard, and onto stone."

"You can wait outside while I check him out, *per favore*," the doctor said, in his careful English. "It is better."

Josselyn agreed that it was. She let herself out of the small medical office that must once have been the house's front room. Outside, the dark had fallen. She sat down on the step and looked around without seeing much of anything, possibly breathing fully for the first time since Cenzo had kissed her.

Since Cenzo had walked into the cottage in Maine.

She shifted, realizing her phone was still in her back pocket, and pulled it out so she could be more comfortable. But then it was in her hand, so she switched it back on and the screen lit up, reality returning in a rush with each incoming text, email, and message.

He had taken her to the castle to isolate her. But now he was out of commission, or at least slowed down.

Josselyn looked back at the door to the doctor's office, where Cenzo was now receiving appropriate medical attention. Then back at her phone, which represented freedom. Or at least, the means to put some distance between her and this man who wanted to maroon her on an island until she became an oversexed Stepford wife.

She swiped through to find a map, so she could see where she was. And there was something about that little dot, blinking at her. Telling her that she was right here, in a coastal village only a bit of a drive up the coast from an airport. Here, not imprisoned on a rock in the sea, firmly entrenched in Cenzo's clutches.

*You are here*, the dot seemed to say. *And you are* you, *still, despite his best efforts.*

Josselyn hooked her free hand over the nape of her neck, squeezing as if that might do something for the tension there. Then she took a few breaths, trying to reset herself. She could still see him falling backward. And that look on his face—not fear or panic, because he was still Cenzo. If anything, he had looked thunderstruck that gravity dared to assert itself upon him.

She almost found that funny now.

Josselyn wanted to call her father to assure him that she was all right, but it occurred to her as she swiped through to her contacts that she had more pressing things to worry about now. First, her father would assume that she was all right, so calling to tell him she was would necessitate telling him what had transpired. And she couldn't bring herself to break his heart over the phone. Second, and more pressing, Cenzo was likely to wake up fully at any moment, shake himself off, and come after her.

She had absolutely no doubt about that.

And so she had to question why she was sitting there on an old step in this tiny village, wasting precious moments, when what she could be doing was putting space between her and him.

No matter how he tasted. Or how that magical fire seemed to dance in her still.

*Focus*, she ordered herself.

Over the next half hour or so, out there in an ancient street, she made arrangements as swiftly as possible. At any moment she expected the door behind her to fly open, and the doctor and his nurse to come out, exclaiming the name Falcone to the night sky. It was inevitable, and that meant, ring in her pocket or not, Josselyn needed an escape route.

But when the door opened, it was only the doctor's wife, and she was smiling. A very soothing, professional sort of smile that was not remotely tainted with the sort of awe and reverence the name Cenzo Falcone generally inspired.

Josselyn smiled back, and hoped she looked… Well, whatever would be appropriate if she hadn't just put into motion an escape plan while her husband of less than a day lay in an exam room nearby with a head injury.

"He's looking much better," the woman said, more in Italian than English, but she spoke slowly enough that Josselyn could pick it up well enough. "But he is, how you say, he does not…" She pointed at herself, moving her finger over her face. "He cannot say who he is."

Josselyn nodded, trying to look serious. When secretly, she was perhaps slightly relieved that it sounded like he'd hurt his jaw in the fall. Which would save her his scathing remarks.

"You could take him to hospital," the woman continued. "In Taormina."

"He really can't speak?"

"Confused," the woman said, then shrugged, indicating with some pantomime that Josselyn should follow her inside.

Josselyn responded with even more pantomime that she would follow in a moment, pointing at her phone. She considered her options when the door closed, leaving her outside again, and as she did an SUV pulled up before her. And behind it, another vehicle, but this one with rental hire information on its side.

"You made it here so quickly," she said to the driver of the SUV. "I'm very impressed."

*"Grazie,"* the man said, smiling broadly. "It was nothing."

Because it turned out that when offered an incredible gratuity on top of an already expensive request for speed, people were only too happy to oblige.

"Hold on one moment," she told him, calculating possibilities as quickly as she could. "I might have another job for you. Is that okay?"

The driver assured her that it was more than okay, so Josselyn turned and went back inside the doctor's office.

She braced herself for a round of questions and accusations about what it was she was doing with a man as easily recognizable as Cenzo Falcone, but when she pushed her way into the exam room, the doctor only smiled and asked her to step back out so they could discuss his condition.

Josselyn took a moment, looking past the doctor to where Cenzo stared back at her, his eyes open and an expression she could not possibly begin to categorize in those ancient eyes of his.

She shivered as she followed the doctor into the next room.

"He is awake now, this is good," the older man told her. "It is my opinion that if you watch him tonight and make sure there is no concussion and no more unconsciousness, maybe no hospital is necessary. Where did this happen? On your little sailboat?"

"Oh," she said airily, not sure why something in her cautioned her against telling the truth. "We made a day out of it. A pretty sail, stopping along the way to climb on rocks and things."

She expected the doctor to question her further on that, but he only nodded. "The concern is that he slipped in and out of consciousness a few times. Maybe this could happen again. At the hospital, they will be able to monitor him, make sure that all he suffers is this bruise, you understand."

"I thought he was confused, too?"

"He didn't want to tell us his name." But the doctor shrugged. "There are many people who react like this when they wake up to find themselves somewhere strange. Maybe this is nothing."

What it sounded like to Josselyn was that the mighty Cenzo Falcone did not wish it to be known that he had been laid low in this fashion. No doubt his ego wouldn't allow it. She nodded sagely. "My car is outside, so it will be easy enough to transport him. I really can't thank you enough for your help. What do I owe you?"

The older doctor looked as if he couldn't decide whether to be insulted or amused. "This is not necessary. We are in Italia, *sì*? He is okay, this is the important thing."

Josselyn thanked him, and then there was nothing to do—especially as the doctor and his wife gazed at her so expectantly—but step back into the exam room.

And face Cenzo at last.

He was sitting up on the side of the bed, that livid, darkening bruise doing nothing to dim the ferocity of his gaze. He looked rumpled and impatient and alarmingly sexy, and it was that last part that she was going to have to come to terms with, Josselyn knew. But not here. Not now. Not until she handled the details of this as any decent person would, and then made good her escape.

"There's a car for you outside," she told him in as steady a voice as she could manage. "It will take you to the hospital. Or wherever you want to go, if the standard of care at the Taormina hospital is not to your liking."

Cenzo continued to stare at her, looking more and more thunderous by the moment. He swallowed, as if his throat was dry. Then his head tilted slightly to one side, and she could tell by how gingerly he did it that even that little movement hurt him.

Josselyn supposed she was a great fool, because she didn't like to think of him hurting. It made her stomach go hollow again. Even when she knew that his entire aim where she was concerned was to make sure she hurt. And, through her, to hurt her father too.

*Well*, she told herself tartly, *you might not get applause for being the bigger person, but that doesn't mean you shouldn't do it anyway.*

And maybe, she thought then, he hadn't been as off base with his comments about her martyr complex as she'd wanted to imagine.

He was continuing to stare at her in that same way, as if he couldn't make sense of her, and it made her uneasy. Or anyway, that was how she chose to interpret the spike of heat and sensation low in her belly.

"It's encouraging that you're sitting up," she said brightly. "I thought for a moment there that you'd suffered something truly terrible, like a spinal injury. But that doesn't seem to be the case, thank goodness."

Cenzo's head tilted again, slightly more. Just slightly.

"I have no idea who you are." And his tone was accusing, as if it was clear to him that she'd done something to him. He shook his head slightly, then winced. "But perhaps this is of no matter, because I do not seem to know who I am, either."

Josselyn could not have heard that correctly. "What do you mean? Exactly?"

He made an expression of distaste, and the impatience she'd seen in his expression intensified. "What I said. You are looking at me and speaking to me as if you know me, but I am certain I have never seen you before. And when the doctor asked me my name, I opened my mouth to tell him but nothing came to mind. Can you explain this?"

And wasn't that the Cenzo Falcone experience in a nutshell, Josselyn thought as she tried to take that in. The man had woken up to find himself in a medical facility with no memory, and his first reaction was not fear or concern. Perish the thought! He instead demanded that others provide him with explanations.

"All right," she said as calmly as she could. "That's a curveball, certainly. What do you remember?"

He considered, then slowly shook his head—wincing once again, as if he'd forgotten he was hurt. "It is as if it is on the tip of my tongue, yet nothing comes. As if I need to concentrate, but when I do, there is nothing. A blankness."

"Nothing at all?" Her pulse picked up and ran. "Not even a shred of something?"

"I know I am speaking English to you, though I

spoke Italian to the doctor," he said, his tone withering. Apparently that much was innate. He gestured at his own torso. "I know that I am fit and in excellent health. The doctor told me we were sailing and I can picture sailboats, the sea, beaches and tides…" He lifted a shoulder. "But none of it is specific. None of it is mine."

Josselyn's heart was beating much too fast. Of all the things she'd worried might happen, this hadn't rated so much as a stray thought. Because it was madness. So mad she almost thought he had to be faking it to see what she would do…

Except she couldn't imagine any scenario in which Cenzo Falcone would pretend for even one moment to be anything less than what he was. To appear in any way impaired, or seemingly helpless—not that he was acting as if he was either of those things.

On the contrary, he was lounging there on a hospital bed as if he believed that if he simply made enough demands of her, he would remember himself.

"Clearly you know more than I do," he said then, again with that note of accusation and a banked fury in his old coin gaze. "Perhaps you would do me the favor of telling me something. Like my name."

Only this man would wake with amnesia and fail to find the experience even remotely humbling. Josselyn almost wanted to laugh.

"Your name is Cenzo," she told him, and she expected to see a light bulb go off in him. She expected to see the centuries of Falcone arrogance slam back into place. She watched those eyes of his, waiting for them to change from simply cool and watchful to that full-on predator's stare that made her shiver just thinking about it.

"Cenzo," he repeated, as if trying out the name. "I assume that is short for Vincenzo? I do not feel as if I am a man with a nickname, if I am honest. It seems… Beneath me."

*Of course it does*, Josselyn thought. And managed, somehow, to keep from rolling her eyes.

"I have no idea if it's a nickname or not," she told him. He had a great many names, after all. Who was to say that Cenzo wasn't one of them? She hadn't been paying close attention during that part of their wedding ceremony. She had been far too busy ordering herself to stand still and look graceful, rather than turning on her heel and bolting back down the aisle to get away from him.

"The doctor made it sound as if you were my wife," Cenzo said, a heavy kind of disapproval all over him. Because along with the accusation and arrogance, he had apparently remained judgmental, too. "Can this be so if you know so little about your own husband?"

And Josselyn's heart beat even faster. She felt herself grow warm, but this time, not because of anything he was doing. But because of her own audacity.

Because she couldn't seem to stave off the truly insane idea that had come to her. And no matter how she tried to push it aside, it seemed to grow larger and wider inside her.

Until it was all she could think about.

Because if ever there was a man on this earth who deserved a little bit of humbling, it was this one.

She stared back at him, her mind racing. She would have to rent an actual motorboat, or buy one, whatever. That way, she could monitor him herself and if there was trouble, get him back to land more quickly. That was the main thing.

*Are you really debating doing this?* a voice inside her asked. *You know it's wrong.*

She did. But maybe there were degrees of wrong. Because she had not signed up to be the object of his unhinged revenge conspiracies. And yet he had carried her off to that ruin of a rock, mocked and threatened her, and had been very explicit about what he planned to do to her while she was there.

And she believed that if he hadn't fallen, he would have set about doing exactly what he'd promised. He had already been doing it, she thought, remembering that kiss.

So really, what was the harm in turning the tables?

Unlike him, she had no intention of actually hurting anyone. Unlike him, she had no ulterior motive. This was an opportunity for the great Cenzo Falcone to see the world a little bit differently, for a change. That was all.

Maybe, she told herself piously, it might even make him a better person. In the end.

She couldn't deny that beyond all of that, she would certainly enjoy watching her powerful, overwhelming husband cut down to palatable size.

"Well?" he demanded. "Have you anything to say for yourself?"

And that sealed it, really. Because even now, when he had no idea who she was, what the relationship was, or even who *he* was, that was how he spoke to her. As if she owed him her instant obedience.

Oh, yes, she was definitely going to enjoy this.

And she would worry, later, about how it made her a terrible person.

She would worry later—when their month on that rock was up, no real harm was done, and maybe, just maybe, the vainglorious Cenzo Falcone had learned a lesson.

"I'm afraid the doctor put ideas in your head," she said, and smiled. "And because you've been banged up today, I will forgive it. But you do not normally speak to me in this manner, Cenzo."

She already enjoyed it. That was the truth of it.

She already wanted to laugh out loud, she enjoyed it so much.

Instead, Josselyn held his gaze. "You're my servant."

# CHAPTER SEVEN

TRY AS HE WOULD, Cenzo could not seem to access the great and abiding joy his employer told him he had once possessed in his job. In his life, which apparently demanded total immersion in that job.

"I have never met a happier servant," the *signora* had told him merrily while his head had still been pounding in that doctor's office. "You have often told me that you could not think of a single thing you would prefer to do. And, sure enough, your joy infused every moment of your day, every task you completed, everything you said and did."

A week later, Cenzo could not imagine how that could ever have been so. He felt a great many things as he sank back into his role, but none of them were joy.

Or even adjacent to joy, by his reckoning.

They had not gone to the hospital in Taormina. His employer had waved a breezy hand and told him that she would be happy to monitor him herself, unless, of course, he had a driving need to seek hospital attention, in which case she would have him transported down the coast at once. And Cenzo did not have to dig particularly deeply to feel that he did not have any such need.

His head had hurt that first day. There'd been a ringing in his ears, that pounding, and a headache every time he so much as drew breath, it seemed. When they'd left the doctor's office, she'd encouraged him to get into the back seat of the SUV that waited for her and had left him there a moment while she conferred with the driver. No doubt he should have listened to the conversation. He should have tried to glean any information he could about the bewildering state he found himself in.

But instead, he'd simply…sat there. And had the distinct sensation that allowing another to cater to him while he remained in the dark was new to him, in some way.

Which would make sense as a servant, he supposed.

They'd driven down to the water, where the *signora* had a boat waiting. A boat she piloted, only waving him off when he suggested that perhaps he ought to do the honors. For surely that was his role.

"Who knows if you remember how to operate a boat?" she'd asked in her merry way. "I'd rather not discover that you don't remember a thing while we're in the open water, if you don't mind."

He had felt as if he ought to argue about that, but hadn't.

And then she'd taken him across the water to a desolate slab of rock topped with ruins, where, she claimed, they would remain for a month.

He had helped as best he could—happy that the painkillers the doctor had given him had kicked in—while she brought the boat into the rocky, unwelcoming shore, then moved it back out again while towing the waiting rowboat. She'd thrown down an anchor and then had made as if to row them to shore.

Cenzo had drawn the line at that. He might have been wounded. And a joyful servant. But he was still a man.

He had done the rowing.

But it was when she started to lead him up the stairs that seemed to march on into forever, and rather steeply, that he was so dubious he'd had no choice but to share it. As perhaps servants did not usually do.

"This is a place you choose to come?" he had asked. "Deliberately?"

The *signora* had gazed at him serenely from two narrow steps above, putting her just below his eye level. "Oh, indeed. It has been in my husband's family for many generations. It's an excellent place to…" She had smiled widely. "Rediscover oneself."

Perhaps that made this the perfect place, Cenzo

had thought, for a man as adrift as he was then. Though he could not pretend that anything about it *felt* perfect. Particularly not when the place was nothing but the remains of something better.

But his was not to reason why, he had tried to remind himself as they had climbed. His was to... *serve*, apparently.

He had tried to allow the notion of service to sink into him like the sun. To warm inside him and become...well, palatable, anyway.

When they made it up flight after flight of winding old stairs that wound around and around the isolated rock, he had found he liked the newer part of the castle much better. The ruins made him uneasy. It was as if they whispered secrets of other forgotten lives, drawing comparisons he did not wish to entertain. Cenzo vastly preferred the sleek lines of the renovated part. He would not have said that it felt like a *homecoming*, exactly, but for the first time since he'd woken up in that exam room, he had breathed easier.

That had made him feel as if he was moving in the right direction, no matter what else might have been happening. It had felt like progress.

"You must have a splitting headache," the *signora* had said as they stood in the grand foyer, all clean lines interrupted with a bold wall here, a commanding piece of art there. "Why don't you head to the kitchen and get something to drink? I'm sure I have some headache tablets that I can give you."

She had pointed in the correct direction, and Cenzo had obediently taken himself off to a kitchen he was pleased to find was as sleek and welcoming as the rest. He had still found it difficult to imagine himself *serving* in any capacity, but he took it as a good sign that the kitchen felt like his. The whole renovated part of the castle did, come to that. But then, he was sure he had read once—back behind that wall in his head that he couldn't penetrate— that good servants felt that kind of ownership over the places where they served. He had the dim impression of a film featuring stately British homes and some kind of saturnine-faced butler.

He had found all the glasses in precisely the place he imagined they ought to be, for his convenience, and that, too, seemed to indicate that he had indeed spent time in this place.

It seemed to take the *signora* a great long while to locate her medicine. When she'd come back, she had seemed faintly flushed. As if she'd exerted herself in the search for paracetamol. He had opened his mouth to inquire, but had closed it again.

Surely servants did not last long in their positions if they asked such personal questions of their employers. Maybe he'd picked that up in the film, too.

She had slid the bottle over to him, smiling again. And he had admitted, then, that despite the racket in his head, he liked the way she smiled. Too much, perhaps.

"Why don't you take the rest of the night off?" she had asked. "And tomorrow as well. If you like, we can set you up in the master bedroom, because I really don't like to think of you sleeping as you usually do when you're trying to recover from something as traumatic as this has been."

He had tossed back a couple of tablets and swallowed them down without water. "How is it that I usually sleep?"

Again, she had smiled. Angelically, he had thought.

"You prefer a pallet on the floor. That seems austere to me, but you've always claimed that you feel better that way. You don't like to coddle yourself. Strength of body and strength of mind breeds strength of character, you always say."

Cenzo had thought he sounded like a bit of an ass, but kept that to himself.

"I will remain in my usual place, I think," he had said, more forbiddingly than he should have, given that she was his employer. He had tried to look… servile. "And hope it encourages my memory to return more quickly."

And he had thought she looked almost guilty then, but he'd supposed that was his headache, obscuring everything.

When she had led him upstairs, the room that

was designated as his looked like it might once have been a sitting room of some kind, though it featured only chairs and a table. No sofa. Not even a settee. There were suitcases stacked neatly in one corner and on the floor beneath the windows, a single pillow and a pile of nicely folded blankets.

Austere, indeed.

"Don't hesitate to call for me if you need something," she had said.

"I will, *signora*," he had replied.

Though he had privately thought that he would rather die than do any such thing.

He had lain down and pulled the blankets over him, then had waited for his body to relax into what it surely knew, no matter what he remembered. And instead had seemed able to think only of how hard the stones were beneath him.

But as the days passed, he became used to them. And to his little pallet beneath the window.

What he did not get used to in any hurry was his job. Or, as the *signora* told it, his *calling*. More than a career. More than simply something he did for money—assuming he had money out there somewhere.

But no matter how he searched within himself, Cenzo couldn't seem to find anything that resonated with that.

Still, he performed the duties expected of him. He found that he enjoyed cooking in that kitchen where he felt most like himself, whoever that was. He appreciated the excellent ingredients available to him and the greatest pleasure, he found as he compiled ingredients, was serving what he made to the *signora*.

Cleaning, on the other hand, he found distasteful in the extreme. And worse than that, simply tedious. Cenzo could not reconcile the joy he'd been told he'd once felt in performing these tasks with the boredom he felt while doing them now.

Sometimes it felt more like rage than boredom, but he did it all the same.

"Why don't you join me?" the *signora* asked one evening after he'd brought her the small feast he'd prepared. She nodded when he looked at her in surprise. "It seems silly for you to sit in the kitchen, eating by yourself when it is only the two of us here. You might as well enjoy this view too, especially since we are both eating at the same time."

Something in him had turned over at that, though he could not have said what it was.

But when he retrieved a place setting and his own meal, then sat down with her, it felt as if something in him…settled.

Had they eaten in this manner before? Was it a habit? Or was it more of an employer's whim, that she could carry out or not as she saw fit?

He thought he probably had his answer with that last one.

"Your ring is very beautiful," he said, because she was holding her wineglass before her and the ring caught the setting sun, sending it dancing all around them in shards of light. She looked startled, looking down at the enormous ring as if she didn't know how it had gotten on her finger. "Your husband is very generous."

"I suppose he is," she agreed. "But he is...complicated."

"All men are complicated," Cenzo replied. "Men like to claim they are simple, but it is a mask. Where it counts, they are always layered."

She seemed to take a long time to look up at him again. "Are you remembering?"

He laughed at that, then wondered if servants weren't meant to laugh when she seemed to react to the sound. Cenzo cleared his throat. "I remember nothing. But I feel certain, nonetheless."

The *signora* looked back at her ring, giant and blue, like a pool she wore on her hand. He was surprised he hadn't noticed it that first night in the doctor's office, because he'd certainly noticed it every day since.

"I think it is people who are complicated," she was saying. "And never more complicated than in the ways they interact with each other."

He thought it ought to have made him feel any number of things that he could not remember his own relationships. He felt certain, yet again, that he'd had them—even if he couldn't remember any details. In the next moment he knew that was true, because he remembered having sex. Not specifically. Not attached to any particular woman's face, but he knew. He remembered that much.

As did his sex, he discovered the next moment, when the *signora* lifted her face to look at him again and the setting sun made her gleam like honey.

*Josselyn.* The name bloomed inside him as if he had always known it. *Her given name is Josselyn.*

He grew harder, and understood exactly what the ache in him was, then. "Perhaps complication is a compliment," he said when he could speak without all that *wanting* in his voice. Or he hoped he could. "If relationships were simple, they would be boring, would they not?"

Josselyn seemed to have shadows on her face, or maybe it was the night drawing close at last, after another stunning blue Mediterranean day. "We wouldn't want that. Anything but boredom."

In his pallet, later, after she'd gone up to her room at the top of the tower, Cenzo found himself thinking far too much about this woman he lived with. And served. And had broken bread with tonight.

And wanted terribly, like a fever in his blood.

She was the most beautiful woman he had ever seen. He laughed as he thought that, because he couldn't remember any others, but even so, he was sure that if he could personally remember the faces of every woman he'd ever encountered she would still blow them all away.

The sun moved all over her the way he wanted to do. Cenzo found himself jealous of the *sun*.

*Josselyn*, he thought, her name like a song in him.

As the days passed, he found he focused on her more and more. Some days he thought he could almost taste her. Some nights he dreamed of kissing her, and there was something about those dreams that made him wake, panting. Hard as a spike. Desperate, which he sensed was not his typical state.

He often toyed with the heavy ring on his finger in the dark, finding it hard to believe that he had ever made the vow of celibacy Josselyn had told him he had.

"I find that doubtful," he had said when she shared this amazing revelation with him. When it had finally occurred to him that if it were a wedding ring, there must have been a wedding. And must therefore be a wife…out there somewhere. A notion that had not sat well with him. "Extremely doubtful, *signora*."

"You truly are a Renaissance man, Cenzo," she had replied, sitting in the little library room in the tower with a book open before her. And surely something was wrong with him that he'd begun to associate that particularly serene smile of hers with information about himself he was not going to like.

"You wear that ring as a celebration of yourself. The commitment you made to *you*."

Josselyn looked as if she thought that was beautiful. Cenzo thought he'd like to punch himself in the face. That was a commitment that he could make to himself. It rather sounded like he needed it.

"How extraordinary," he had said. "I do not feel at all like a monk."

"Do any monks actually *feel* like monks?" she'd asked airily. "It seems to me that's the whole point of becoming one. If the vow was easy to make, would it be worth making?"

Cenzo had not shared his personal opinion, which was that some vows were deeply stupid.

Still other nights he lay awake and lectured himself. He told himself that he ought to be grateful. Because it wasn't as if he remembered any part of the job he'd done here before. Josselyn was constantly reminding him. She was unfailingly nice about it, always kind and patient as she told him he usually did things like gather fresh flowers and festoon them about, or scrub the floors with his own hands as he felt that made them gleam brighter. He knew he should have been far more thankful for her willingness to not simply…have him replaced.

But it turned out he was the sort of monk who struggled mightily with anything like gratitude.

And no matter what, no matter how he tried to trick himself into remembering something that might make sense of these choices he'd made, he always came up against that same wall.

His bruises faded quickly, and that almost made it worse. Because then he simply looked like a normal man, but one who'd been born at the beginning of the month. Fully formed, completely useless, and doomed to be a mystery to himself.

Cenzo felt, strongly, that he was not accustomed to finding himself a cipher.

It was better when he focused on Josselyn rather than himself. And the bonus was, he liked doing exactly that.

Perhaps it was the only thing he enjoyed. And perhaps that was the answer to the puzzle of his identity right there.

"What does your husband do when you take month-long trips to a place like this?" he asked one evening as they sat together in one of the rooms off the kitchen, because the wind had picked up too much to eat outside. She usually came to sit with him in the kitchen as he prepared their dinner each night, and, in turn, he had taken to eating with her all of the time now. It seemed simpler.

And though she hadn't reissued her invitation, she hadn't rescinded it, either.

Once again, Cenzo questioned how it was he had ever taken joy in servitude when he took far too much pleasure in pushing boundaries he shouldn't have.

*Perhaps it is precisely the pushing of these*

*boundaries, with her, that you took pleasure in*, a voice in him countered.

Cenzo had no trouble believing that.

"I believe my husband has an endless capacity for entertaining himself with his own bank balance," Josselyn replied in a darker tone than usual. "Some men are like that. It is about what can be bought and sold, always. That's the pleasure they take in things, if they take any pleasure in anything. And it isn't about money, because believe me, they already have enough."

"Men are hunters." Cenzo shrugged. "What they cannot stalk for their dinner, they must hunt in other ways."

She looked at him curiously. "What do you hunt? Can you remember?"

"I cannot," he said. Yet for once it did not bother him. "But I feel certain that whatever it was, I was very good at it."

He liked the way she laughed then, as if delighted, even though he was baffled by it. For he had come to realize that no matter what, no matter that there was that wall preventing him from remembering the details about his life, he felt very sure about who he was.

Supremely certain.

And as he sat there, thinking about that certainty while Josselyn's laughter made music between them, Cenzo could suddenly triangulate a life that made sense.

Finally.

There was that ring on his finger that Josselyn told him was a vow he had made. There was what she claimed was his commitment to his role here—his service to and for her. And the third point of that triangle, the most important point, was Josselyn herself. His *signora*. The beautiful woman whose laugh was brighter than the sun, and who sometimes smiled at him and made his chest feel too tight.

He could see the purpose in that life. And the beauty in it, too.

And perhaps that was the recipe for joy—maybe even that joy she had told him he had always felt in his work.

Maybe the work was incidental and the point was her.

He felt something in him roar at that, like a dragon, and knew it was the truth.

"It's a good thing that even getting knocked on the head hasn't taken away your sense of yourself," Josselyn said, though she did not sound as if she thought it was all that good.

"Surely losing one's memory should be clarifying." He found himself lounging back in his chair, his gaze on her. "Surely I should become more of who I am, not less."

Her dark eyes seemed particularly mysterious to

him then. "That's the internal debate, isn't it? Some think a person is made of certain immutable characteristics, set in stone at birth. Others are sure it's our experiences that make us who we are. It's the nature versus nurture debate, and I'm not sure either side has ever won it."

"I cannot speak to your philosophy," he replied. "But while I may not recall the details about my life, I find that knowing myself does not appear to pose a challenge."

"You are a man with a singular sense of himself, Cenzo." Her voice was quiet, and she seemed to cling tighter to her wineglass than she usually did. "You always have been."

"And your husband?" he asked. Because it was difficult to recall that she had one, he could admit. He didn't like that she was married. And there seemed no point in pretending that his acceptance of that unworthy thought wasn't also the acceptance of another, even darker truth. He wanted her regardless of her marital status. That was the beginning and the end of it, because she already felt like his. Cenzo could only hope that the things he wanted weren't stamped all over him as he gazed at her. "Surely you must have married him for his own collection of…singular characteristics."

She blinked then, an expression he couldn't read flashing over her face. He thought she looked almost…uneasy. Even upset. But she lowered her lashes and when she lifted them again, the expression was gone as if he'd made it up.

"My husband and I are separated," she told him, her voice sounding odd to his ears. "He is…focused on other things at this time."

"Is that why you are spending a month here?" With him instead of the man she'd married. The one who had a greater claim to her than he did, a notion he did not care for at all. "To find your own focus?"

But she stood then, and he knew that meant she was cutting off this conversation. And right when it had gotten interesting. Sure enough, she smiled in that way he already knew meant she did not intend to continue. Ever.

"I don't know why I mentioned that. It's irrelevant." She cleared her throat, but that smile of hers seemed far less serene than usual. "Good night, Cenzo."

"Good night, *signora*," he replied, because that was the appropriate thing to call her.

Her name was a treasure he hoarded and kept to himself.

Josselyn headed up into the tower, but he lingered in the kitchen long after he'd cleaned away the remnants of their dinner.

It was as he had told her. He couldn't remember the details of his life, but the things he did know were bedrock certainties.

Like this one: Her husband was a fool, but he was not.

And if her husband was not man enough to claim the wife he had, Cenzo saw no reason why *he* should respect such foolishness.

Because he was the one who was here, making Josselyn laugh.

He was the one who tended to her, feeding her and caring for her, day in and day out.

As far as Cenzo was concerned, he was the only husband she needed.

# CHAPTER EIGHT

JOSSELYN COULD NO longer pretend that she was anything but a terrible person.

Some days that weighed heavily on her. Other days, she rationalized that having made the choices she already had, there was no going back without causing even more trouble.

She had felt guilty immediately. The very moment the words were out of her mouth and Cenzo had blinked, clearly trying to imagine himself *a servant*. Josselyn hadn't been able to imagine it herself, really, but she'd said it. There was no taking it back. Surely that would confuse him even more.

That first night, she hadn't slept, because… Had she really told the man to go sleep on the floor with a head injury? Yes, she'd offered him the master bedroom, but she couldn't pretend she hadn't known full well he would refuse. That was why she'd rushed into the tower and moved his things. And surely that level of manipulativeness made her evil. Rotten to the bone, just as he'd believed her father was.

The way she'd told him his mother was, little though he'd wanted to believe her in those last moments he was still himself.

Josselyn thought about that all the time—the poison his mother had fed him that had led him to think his only reasonable course was revenge.

*What do you imagine his reaction will be to* this *act?* her conscience liked to ask her daily. *He might well prefer a dose of poison to scrubbing floors.*

She'd tried to assuage her conscience by surreptitiously checking on him every hour on the hour throughout that first night, and the next few nights as well, just to make sure that her questionable desire to get her own back with him didn't result in any actual health issues on his part.

But he seemed in perfect health save for his lack of memory.

A few days into it, after she'd waved a hand and told him that he liked to clean the castle's many windows every Tuesday, she'd taken the hired boat out again. The helpful driver of the SUV that night in the village had arranged the whole thing for her, only too happy to do what he could after she'd demonstrated that she had unlimited funds at her disposal.

It was even a nice boat, she'd thought that first night, and then again when she took it out once more. Fast enough that she could make it back across the water to Sicily in less than half the time it had taken her to sail. That was good to know. It made her feel much better about choosing not to take Cenzo to the hospital. Once she'd determined that she could get to Taormina fairly quickly if she had to, she'd taken the opportunity to call her father. Just to check in. And to assure all her friends that she was alive and well in her archaic arranged marriage, despite all their proclamations of doom.

When she'd calmed all the nerves she could, she'd spent some time downloading articles on head injuries from the internet so she could make sure that she wasn't irreparably harming the man. And could spot any signs that his health was taking a dive.

As the days passed, Cenzo not only exhibited no signs of decline, he seemed to thrive. More and more by the day. And Josselyn was fascinated that even though he couldn't remember a thing, he was in no way less himself.

Arrogant. Commanding. Steeped in the whole of his glorious history. And quite obviously mystified by the notion that anyone would ever choose to be a servant, which she couldn't help but find entertaining.

*Because you're an awful person*, she would tell herself again and again.

But then she remembered what his plan had been

for their time in this place. The revenge he planned to take on her, thanks to the lies his mother had told him. She knew they were lies. She'd read the woman's letters. And surely even this terrible charade she was inflicting on him was better than *that*. Because *she* wasn't trying to make *him* a slavering addict, so that she would somehow break her own father's heart for more of a taste.

She wasn't trying to *break* him. That was the difference, she assured herself.

Though her conscience wasn't so sure.

"You look distressed," Cenzo said one evening as they sat out on the balcony, though the air was cool. Even here summer waned, however mildly. He indicated the first course that he'd only just brought out, a rich stew of eggplant, pine nuts, and plump, sweet raisins. "I hope it is not the *caponata*."

"Of course not," she replied. "How could it be? Your cooking is marvelous and you know it."

He inclined his head, regally. And despite herself, Josselyn wanted to laugh. Because for all they might have talked about nature versus nurture in their time here, it seemed that Cenzo's sense of himself was truly innate. He simply was that arrogant.

Even as a servant, he behaved like a king.

"And yet you do not look happy, *signora*."

"Is that important to you?"

And then, instantly, she hated herself for asking. Why was she torturing herself? Asking questions that had no answer, because this intent man who cared for her in his own imposing way was not her husband. She was all too keenly aware of that. This was a version of him, but she knew perfectly well that one day Cenzo would remember his true self—or they would leave here and someone would tell him the truth—and he would hate her. The way he had already hated her when he'd married her.

It made her stomach hurt to contemplate.

"It is quite clear that you are the focus of my existence," he said dryly. "How can you doubt it? You are all I remember."

"We'll see how you are in a few weeks." Josselyn tried to sound severe, because she wanted to laugh again and that felt perilous. It felt intimate. She wanted to bask in this version of Cenzo, who looked at her so intensely but clearly without any desire to harm her.

It made her imagine she could see things in those old coin eyes that she knew were never there.

Or wouldn't be there if he was himself again.

She was a terrible person for this. Josselyn knew she was. But the longer it went on, the less she seemed able to help herself. She would lie awake at night in that wide bed, high in the tower, and decide that tomorrow she would pack him up in the boat, take him to a real hospital where they would recognize him at once, and face the truth about what she'd done.

The truth and what would follow it. His condemnation. Possibly his loathing.

But every morning she would wake up and find herself in the alternate reality she'd created. Where beautiful, impossible Cenzo smiled when he saw her. Where he saw to her comfort, inquired about her needs, and more than that, talked to her as if she was a person instead of a tool to wield.

And in that alternate reality, it was far too easy to get caught up in how astonishingly attractive he was, especially when he wasn't seething with buried rage and revenge. How egregiously gorgeous. Especially because this Cenzo seemed to have no notion of how to dress like the richest man in the world. She supposed it was her fault, because she'd never corrected him when he'd appeared in little more than casual trousers and a T-shirt on the first day. She hadn't insisted that he dress like a butler because she'd been far too busy excoriating herself for her lies.

As the days wore on, she almost wished she'd insisted on the formality. Because maybe if she had, she would be able to think of him differently. Instead of catching her breath every time she looked up and saw him studying her. All that intensity and focus of his, and all of it sharply focused on...tending to her happiness.

Ruthlessly.

So implacably that it made her burn and burn.

Josselyn could not say that she was actually happy in this situation. She was far too aware of the game she was playing. And how temporary it all was, whether she was burned alive or not.

Their time here was running out. Their days were numbered.

And because it was temporary—or so she told herself—she permitted herself to enjoy it.

Because this version of her husband was a delight.

He talked to her. He listened to her. He seemed genuinely interested in what she thought, what she said, what she felt about anything and everything.

She knew better, but he made her heart beat funnily when he smiled at her. He plied her with food. He insisted on running her baths. His eyes followed her everywhere. The heat in him found the fire in her, and they both grew hotter by the day.

And even though she knew that he was just a version of Cenzo that she'd created, Josselyn found that she was susceptible all the same.

Because it turned out that the Cenzo who existed without a thirst for revenge was, more or less, pretty much the perfect man.

A man who asked after her family and when she told him of the tragedy that had taken her mother and brother so long ago, had reached over and placed his hand on her arm. A simple expression of solidarity in grief. In loss.

Even though she knew he could not recall his own loss, his own grieving.

It had moved her far more than any words might have.

This version of Cenzo was the man she'd dreamed he might be when she'd allowed herself to hope that she might have what her parents had.

Knowing he would hate that he had fallen so far was like an ache in her, because she knew that if she could, she would keep him this way forever. No matter what that made her. She couldn't unknow such a thing about herself.

"I have been considering the matter closely," he said one day, as they explored the ruins down near the waterline. It had been Josselyn's idea. Because she thought she needed to actually *do something* with all the strange nervous energy inside of her. Before it burst out of her in inappropriate ways. "But I cannot decide if I am a good man or not."

She looked out through a hole in what had once been an outer wall. She saw the sea before her, that impossible blue. And yet more knowable than the man behind her.

"Surely if you question such things, that already makes you better than some."

"Can a man be good if his thoughts are…unworthy?" he asked.

Josselyn wanted to ask him why he paused over

that last word. She glanced back at him, but as usual, his intense focus made her uncomfortable.

*Uncomfortable is not the right word and you know it*, she scolded herself internally. Because what she felt was too hot. Too interested. Too aware that there was no one on this hunk of rock but the two of them, that he was her husband, and that if she wasn't mistaken, the way he looked at her during these lost days of too many lies was lit up with all the same heat and need she felt herself.

Hotter than the Sicilian sun.

"Thoughts are just thoughts," she managed to say, trying to sound philosophical. "It's what you do that matters."

*Indeed it is*, she thought, and didn't quite manage to keep from wincing.

"It's what you do that is judged," Cenzo countered. "But it must begin within, is that not so?"

"I don't know why you're asking me if you already have an answer."

Her trouble was that all of this felt far too cozy. Too revealing. The searching conversations they kept having, too deeply personal even if he couldn't remember why he would never have had them with her before, felt like intimacy.

It felt like she was getting to know him. The *real* him.

She was all too aware how dangerous that line of thinking was.

Because the real Cenzo would loathe this. He would hate her for allowing him to expose himself. Josselyn knew that.

Yet she also knew that the real Cenzo would have taken great pleasure in doing the same thing to her.

So who was she to lecture him on how to be good?

"Maybe you can't remember the details of who you are," she said after a moment, turning her back to the watchful sea. "But maybe you don't need them. Do you have a sense of right and wrong? Do you know how you feel about things? I think the clues to who we are must be wrapped up in that."

"I believe I am a good man," Cenzo said with his typical conviction. But then he paused, studying her, the sun pouring over him like it wanted to hurt her. "Or I would like to be one. But I do not know if every man thinks these things. Perhaps it is no more than a convenient and flattering way to think of oneself."

"I believe that if you want to be a good man, then you can make sure that you are one." Josselyn's chest ached. "No matter what the provocation. No matter your past. No matter what lies have been told."

His copper and gold gaze seemed brighter, then. "Tell me what that entails."

And somehow, without her noticing, he had drawn close. She found her back against that half wall and then there was Cenzo above her, blocking out the sky.

She felt her breath change. She felt everything inside her pull tight, then seem to shimmer.

"It's not a recipe that you can follow," she whispered. "It's life. It's each and every choice you make over time."

Like the choices she was making now. Or not making.

"Maybe it is not that I truly desire to be a good man." His voice was low. His gaze moved over her face, seeming to catch on her lips. On that mark just beside them. "Maybe it is that I wish only to be good for you."

"Cenzo…" she began.

"Let me in, *signora*," he urged her, his voice a dark thread that seemed to wrap all around her, then tug.

Again and again, pulling her to him. Making her want things she shouldn't.

*Why shouldn't you?* something in her asked. *This version of Cenzo would not hurt you. This version would hurt himself first.*

"Let me in," he said again, and his hands were on the wall beside her head. His face was lowered, hovering there just above hers. It would take so very little to surge onto her toes, lift herself up, place her lips on his.

Again. At last.

Some part of her thought she'd earned it. That she deserved a little pleasure here, before reality ruined them all over again.

"Josselyn," he said, and it made a new sort of heat prickle at the back of her eyes, because oh, how she loved to hear her name in his mouth. His perfect mouth. "You must know that all I wish to do is serve you."

And that almost broke her, but it was a gift.

Because it reminded her who they were.

The real Cenzo Falcone had no wish to serve anyone, least of all her.

Even so much as kissing him now would make her no better than he was. The way he'd claimed a kiss on the boat that first morning, the way he'd branded her with it, had told her in no uncertain terms who he was. But that didn't mean she needed to be like him.

She ducked away, out from beneath his arm, her heart pounding so loudly that it echoed back off the ruins. She wouldn't have been surprised if they could hear it all the way across the water in Taormina.

"Is that a bad thing?" he asked, turning so his eyes could follow her, though he stayed where he was. "I would have thought rather the opposite. Who does not wish to be served? In any and all capacities?"

Josselyn wished she could breathe regularly.

She wished she couldn't feel that wildfire slickness between her legs. She wished it didn't seem like he was in control of her body even though he was no longer *this close* to touching her. And hadn't touched her.

And, because he believed himself her servant, might not touch her at all unless she granted him permission.

She couldn't tell anymore which part of that made her shudder, sending all those goose bumps prickling up and down her spine.

"The trouble is that you don't know what you really want," she managed to say. She even sounded vaguely in control of herself. "How could you? You don't know who you really are."

"You have told me who I am." He shrugged, and he looked dangerous and beautiful. Ancient and untouchable, standing here in these ruins where his ancestors had fought and died, lived and loved. She was sure she could feel their ghosts all around them, judging her as harshly as he would. "And I might not know any number of things, *signora*, but I do know that the things I want are not a mystery to me."

"I told you I was married," she said, expecting that to be a dose of cold water on this situation.

But Cenzo only shrugged, the corner of his mouth crooking up. "So you say. You have run away from this husband of yours and isolated yourself here, where no one can reach you. And you took me with you. I cannot say I see this husband of yours as a barrier."

She laughed at that, helplessly, because what else was there to do?

"You may not consider him a barrier," she said, her voice cracking a little. "But believe me, he is a force. When you feel that force, you will think quite differently about all of this."

His smile widened. "I like my chances."

The absurdity was almost too much for her. "Cenzo. This is not something that's going to happen. It wouldn't be right." She rubbed her hands over her face, not the least bit surprised to discover she was shaking. "Weren't you the one who was worried about how to be a good man?"

"I am not so concerned, it turns out." And though the day was blue and clear, Josselyn was sure she could hear thunderstorms brewing in the distance. "Whether you want to admit it or not, *la mia bella signora*, there is a fire between us."

"There may be," she said, because she thought denying it would make him more resolute. And because it might also actually, physically wound her to deny it. "But that doesn't mean we have to let it burn us alive."

"Maybe, Josselyn, I wish to burn."

"I don't."

It was not the first or even the worst of the lies

she had told him, but this one stung. Horribly. Wounding her, just as she'd feared.

And because she was holding on to the faintest shred of virtue here in the middle of this mess she'd made, she made herself turn and walk away.

Before she found she couldn't.

# CHAPTER NINE

As THEIR MONTH on the island wound down, Cenzo discovered, if not quite a joy in his menial tasks, a sense of satisfaction in completing them.

And could not help but feel it as a kind of victory.

He found he liked the simplicity of their days on this rock. He woke on his pallet, which he had come to appreciate. It was always still dark when he rose, and he liked the faint hints of dawn on the other side of the windows as well as the cold stone beneath his bare feet as he moved through the castle. Up and down the many stairs. He liked to run all the steps, twice, before making his way to the kitchen to begin preparing the *signora*'s breakfast.

He brewed strong coffee every morning, then threw together some batter to make the morning buns he knew Josselyn preferred. Particularly as a counterpoint to his rich, bitter coffee.

Of all the tasks he completed in the course of a day, he thought he liked none so much as when

Josselyn wandered into the kitchen, her lovely, soft eyes still shaded with sleep. She always looked so grateful for the coffee he pressed into her hands and the sweet roll he'd made for her that was usually still warm. So grateful that it made him wonder about her. About the life she'd led on the other side of this strange month. About the things he couldn't recall. That such a small thing could bring her such obvious joy seemed to him like some kind of miracle.

He took it as daily evidence of her husband's unsuitability.

A topic he liked to think about a great deal, especially when Josselyn set off for her morning ramble about the ruins. Cenzo spent the mornings cleaning. He started at the top of the tower and worked his way down, and while that was one more area of this life of his that he would not describe as joyful, per se, he had come to find a certain fulfillment in the completion of his daily chores. And he liked that as he did them he could see Josselyn down below, frowning out at the sea as she took her morning constitutional, moving in and around the ancient stones.

He liked to think that what she worried over, as she stared out toward the horizon, was him.

Just as he liked to think that her nights were sleepless as his were, because the fire could be denied but that didn't make the flames any less bright.

"This is our last day here," she told him that morning, a tautness in the way she held herself that he disliked. "Men will come tomorrow to take us back. When they do, things will change."

"What will change?"

Today she had taken her coffee and her bun out to the terrace. It was another warm morning, the sun and the sea in seeming concert, as if the whole world was that same gleaming blue. Just like the blue stone she wore on her hand.

Something in him shifted uneasily as he stared at that stone today. The ring was always commanding, but it seemed to him almost to echo inside him this morning. But he couldn't quite catch hold of it. Like a melody he knew he recognized, though he'd forgotten all the words.

Cenzo concentrated on Josselyn instead.

He had grown to consider himself something of an expert on her expressions. On every stray feeling he could read in those lovely brown eyes of hers or the color in her cheeks. They seemed grave to him today.

"Everything will change," she warned him. "You must prepare for that. Things have been very simple here, but this is not the real world."

"You must tell me what my position is like in the real world, then," he said, not liking the dire way she was speaking—but also not particularly concerned. Let things change. He would remain the same. He was certain of it. "I'm not sure I know what the position of personal manservant typically entails."

Her smile seemed dry, and in any case, went nowhere in her eyes. "I don't think that's a title you're going to embrace."

"Come now, *signora*." And he threw caution to the wind, then. "If you wish to release me from my position, say so. If that is the change you mean. Or I will be forced to think you are running away. That will not make your marriage any better. You must know this."

She swallowed, visibly, but she did not drop her gaze.

"I had hoped that your memory would come back while we were here," she said, evenly enough. And he might have thought that his words had not affected her at all were it not for the pulse he could see beating out a mad rhythm in her neck. He liked that. He took some pride in it. "I hoped that you would not have to face reality without knowing who you really are."

"You are more concerned with who I really am than I have ever been." He could have sat with her at the little table, but he felt too…restless. That near-melody in his head was driving him a little bit mad. He leaned against the rail instead. "To be perfectly honest with you, I do not care at all what or if I remember. I know what I need to know."

"I think that's easy for you to say that now," she replied, sounding…cautious. "Because you don't know."

"This is what I know about myself, *signora*." He had started calling her that because it had seemed appropriate. It was a reasonable way to address the lady of the house. Or the castle, in her case. But he had come to like the way it tasted on his tongue. And better still the way that each time he said it, she always reacted. A widening of her eyes, a darkening of all that brown. A sucked-in breath, or her lower lip suddenly pulled between her teeth. Oh, yes, he liked it. "I am strong. I sleep upon stones and rise refreshed. At first it seemed to me that a life of servitude must be demeaning, but I have not found it so. There can be no shame in it. Everything I do here, I do well. What have I to fear from a reality that can only offer me more opportunities to excel?"

Josselyn laughed the way she did sometimes, as if she couldn't quite believe the things he said. As if she couldn't quite believe *him*, though that didn't make any sense.

"What's remarkable is that I know you believe this. You might even be right. Still, I know things that you don't know. And, Cenzo, there's no telling what kind of reaction you'll have when you learn them."

She looked so serious that he almost wanted to ask her more questions. To find out what she meant.

But he dismissed the urge almost at once. Because what did he care? He couldn't remember it anyway. He had vague impressions of what the world out there contained. When Josselyn had told him they were off the coast of Sicily, he had known not only what Sicily itself was, but other things about it too. That it sat off the coast of Italy. That it was a part of the Mediterranean region. Over the course of this month, with the help of some of the books in that small library, he'd assured himself that while he might not know himself, he knew the world.

He did not know how to tell her that he was not so concerned with what the world might show him. He was far more convinced that he would be the reckoning upon the world. But saying such things could only sound arrogant, coming as they did from a manservant.

Her manservant.

Josselyn had told him all along that what he did mattered far more than what he thought. That was how he decided, there and then, in the glare of their final morning and her dark predictions about what waited for them when they left this island, that he might as well do what he had wanted to do all along.

"Enjoy your morning," he told her. "And let me worry about the things I will learn tomorrow. There can be no need to ruin our last day on the island, can there?"

She looked torn. She even opened her mouth as if she was about to tell him something important, but stopped herself.

He waited. Because, for her, he would always wait.

"Cenzo…" she began again, but when he only raised a brow, she shook her head.

Then left him there, going off on her morning walk.

It was a longer one today, but that gave him more time to prepare her lunch. And his plans. When she walked back up he met her in the courtyard, carrying a large basket with a thick blanket over one arm.

"What's that?" she asked.

"I thought we should have a picnic."

Josselyn moved her sunglasses to her head, anchoring back her thick, glossy hair. She was wearing one of her dresses today, a short-sleeved, pretty punch of color that ended far enough above her knees to make him feel the fire of her, everywhere.

But the look she trained on him was questioning. "Is that a joke?"

"Am I a man who makes jokes?" His voice was dry. "I cannot remember, but I rather think not."

She smiled. "No, indeed. You are many things, but I've never known you to be a comedian."

"Then perhaps you should accept that I have packed a small feast and intend to feed it to you in the open air, complete with a lovely view of the sea."

And it occurred to him after he set off, taking the stairs that wound not toward the ruins, but toward the back of the rocky island, that he was once again acting as if he was the one in charge rather than her.

He could admit that it felt more natural to him.

Cenzo felt that strange echo again, but shook it off.

And besides, Josselyn followed him. That told him she couldn't be too concerned that he had ideas above his station.

The spot he had in mind was a rocky outcropping, nestled slightly below where the first castle must have stood. It was accessible only by the stairs he took to reach it, carved into a smooth fall of rock with a sheer drop to the sea below.

"I don't ever come this way," she said from behind him. "Probably because it's terrifying."

"You will live, *cara mia*, I promise."

It was not until he'd walked a bit more, with only her shocked silence behind him, that Cenzo realized he had used an endearment. That it had just… slipped out. And it was certainly not the way a manservant addressed his mistress.

But he could hear her feet against the stones. She was still following him. He might have breached the rules of proper etiquette, but it hadn't turned her away.

The trouble was that every time Josselyn failed to put him in his place, he only felt bolder.

It was as well that this was their last day here, then. Better they should sort out what was between them alone, here, before the world intervened.

Before there were external reminders of the difference in their stations.

The outcropping had a thick wall behind it where flowers had grown over time, spilling down from above like a curtain of bougainvillea. And there were stones marking the cliff's edge, making it less dangerous than it might have been otherwise.

"What do you think this was used for?" Josselyn asked as she stopped in the middle of the wide ledge, her gaze out on the ocean before them.

"A lookout station, I imagine," he replied without thinking about it. It was only when she turned to look at him that he realized he'd said that with perfect authority. As if he knew.

He took a moment to examine himself, and it was true. He knew it. "Does that qualify as a memory? I feel certain I am right about this place. It feels like a fact."

"Why don't we call it a fact, then."

And she smiled at him.

That damned smile. It was the ruin of a man, though Cenzo felt nothing like ruined. She smiled at him and his heart danced in his chest. She smiled and the sea and sky seemed to tangle around each other, changing places and he hardly cared.

She smiled and the world stopped dead. And he had to believe that even once they left this place, it would be the same.

And what could he care about the world when he had her?

Because there were whole worlds in this woman, and he wanted to know each and every one of them.

Cenzo spread out the blanket he'd brought, then set about unpacking the lunch he'd made them.

"This isn't a lunch," she said admiringly, coming over to drop down to her knees on the edge of the blanket. "It truly is a feast."

*"Mangia,"* he murmured.

He threw himself down on the blanket, stretching out on his side. And he watched as Josselyn helped herself to the food he'd prepared for her. Cured meats and hard cheeses, piled high, *arancini*, fried balls of creamy risotto, *busiate al pesto Trapanese*, the Sicilian version of pesto with a favorite local pasta shaped like a coil. And a tower of his handmade *cannoli* to finish.

Cenzo liked watching her as she filled her plate, and then, better still, while she ate. Josselyn was not missish, or overly delicate. She wasn't afraid to eat with her fingers, or lick them, or sigh lustily when the flavors overtook her.

He found all of it almost unbearably erotic.

"Why aren't you eating?" she asked. "I hope you don't think that will keep me hanging back politely. It's all too good. Must be the sea air."

"Must be," he agreed.

And he would have eaten, but he wasn't hungry. Or not for the food he had prepared, anyway.

"When is the last time you went on a picnic?" he asked. "It appears to make you giddy."

Josselyn frowned as if she meant to argue, but then the frown melted into a smile. "I don't know that I've ever been on a picnic. This might actually be my first time."

"Then you should be celebrated." Cenzo sat up and pulled out the bottle of wine he had brought, bubbly and sweet, much like she was today.

"Oh, I couldn't possibly," she began, already frowning.

But she went quiet, her cheeks flushed red, when he handed her a glass.

Cenzo lifted his glass in a toast, and the clink of the glasses together shot through him like yet another echo of the song he surely should have known by now.

But that was one more thing he could not bring himself to care about, not when his *signora*, his Josselyn, was sitting there before him, her bare legs kicked out in front of her and her shoes tossed off to one side. The breeze played with her hair the way he wanted to, lifting strands here and there and making her beauty seem all the more impossible.

"You will forgive me," he began, though at that moment he didn't care if she did. Even if he knew she would object, Cenzo needed to say it. "But you are the most beautiful woman I have ever seen."

She laughed, but her cheeks got brighter. "I am the only woman you've ever seen, as far as you know."

"Not true," he argued. "There was another woman. At the doctor's."

"Fair enough." Josselyn rolled her eyes. "I will accept that of the two women you remember seeing, you find me more beautiful than the one old enough to be your mother."

"I dream about you," he told her, keeping his eyes fixed on her face. And ignoring the tightness in his chest. "Then I wake to you each morning and the waking is better than what I dream at night."

Josselyn made a soft, sighing sound, and set her glass down on the blanket between them. "You shouldn't say these things. You can't mean them. You have no context."

"You keep telling me what I *might* feel. What I *might* know. Sometime in the future, perhaps. But I can tell you what I know now." Cenzo felt that echo in him again, but it felt like her. As if she was inside of him. "You, Josselyn. Everything in me is filled with you."

He thought she looked anguished. He watched, everything in him hectic, as she got to her feet. He liked the way she moved even now, lithe and easy. She moved to the rocks at the cliff's edge and he took a moment to appreciate the picture she made there, her hair blown back, her dress moving over her body, as she stared out into eternity.

Only then did he follow her. He came to stand behind her, close enough that her hair danced over him at last.

"I may not know who I was two months ago, but I know you," he said, his mouth at her ear. "I know you want me, Josselyn. It is written all over you. Every time you look at me. Every time you smile, or laugh. I don't need to remember anything when you are before me. I can see all the things I want as if they are emblazoned upon you."

"Wanting something doesn't mean you should have it," she said, though her voice was low. And he could feel the tremors that went through her, one after the next.

"Why shouldn't you have it?" he demanded. Then his hands were on her, taking her by the shoulders and turning her to face him. There was a kind of misery in her gaze, and he couldn't stand it. He couldn't bear it. "I do not wish to be cruel, but if this upset is for your husband, you must forget him. What kind of man allows his wife to go off with another man and live like this for a month?"

Josselyn was shaking her head. "Even if I told you everything that I know about you, don't you see? It would only be a story you were told. It would mean nothing."

"Let us write our own story," he said.

And then he could wait no longer.

Cenzo lowered his mouth to hers, and finally—*finally*—took her lips.

And kissed her as if his life depended on it.

It did, somehow. He was sure of it.

And it was a marvel of sensation. He felt exhilarated. As if he'd come home at last.

Better still, that fire between them ignited.

He thought she might pull away and run from him once more, but instead, she melted against him. And then, when he angled his head so he could taste her deeper, wilder, she surged against him, wrapped her arms around his neck, and threw gas straight into the flames.

Cenzo kissed her again and again, then had the presence of mind to scoop her up into his arms and carry her back over to the blanket. He lay her down in the middle, like she was one more dessert. A sweet banquet for him to enjoy.

He came down with her, every part of his body tight with need and wonder, because she was finally in his arms. *Finally.*

"I shouldn't let this happen," she whispered, though she made no move to get up.

"I want you," he told her, though it was more than that.

His heart was involved, and every bone in his body, and every last part of him—from his dreams at night to his every waking thought. But he worried that if he called it what it was, she would balk.

"I want you," he said again, as if it was a vow. "And I cannot imagine there is any knowledge on this earth that could change that."

Then he set his mouth to hers again before she could argue, kissing her until she was pliant and soft. And for a lifetime or two they were tangled together like that in the open air, as if they were a part of the sea and the sky at last.

And it was true that he couldn't quite remember other women, but that didn't mean Cenzo didn't know precisely what to do. He pressed openmouthed kisses down the length of her neck, so he could set his mouth to that pulse that always betrayed her.

His hands skimmed down the front of her body, finding her curves and then making his way to the hem of that flirty little dress so he could do the whole of it in reverse. But this time with his palm touching her warm flesh and exulting in it.

He found her hip, then her breasts, and he could bear that only for a moment before he pulled back from her, stripping the dress up and over her head and tossing it aside. She wore a lacy little half bra that lifted her breasts to him as if on platters.

This banquet, he could not deny. Cenzo bent his head to taste her, to devour her.

To worship her.

And the first time she shattered, it was like that,

her back arched and her nipple in his mouth while he played with the other, using her body like it was an instrument.

His instrument, playing his tune, at last.

Her moans licked all over him, spurring him on. He found the shallow dent of her navel, then moved even farther down to bite gently at one hip and to grip the other, his fingers wrapping around to test her plump behind. He spread her out before him, using his shoulders to keep her legs apart.

And he liked that she wore another little scrap of lace there, just covering her sex.

He followed suit, covering her mound with his open mouth, sucking gently on the lace until her cries changed pitch.

Cenzo stripped the panties off her hips and down her legs, then settled himself back into place. He drew her perfectly formed legs over his shoulders, lifting her up on the shelf of his hands and licking his way into all her soft heat.

She tasted even better than he could have imagined—and he had done little but imagine it this whole month. He found the center of her need and played with it, taking his time to find what made her jolt, what made her cry out. He filed away every buck of her hips, every arch of her back.

He learned her. All of her.

Cenzo brought her to the edge, then receded. Over and over, until she was sobbing out his name, throwing it out into the sky above them, the sea beyond.

And only when her fingers were sunk as deep into his hair as they could get and her hips seemed to rise of their own accord, did he finally take her over.

He held her there, still shattering and shattering around him, until he thought that his own greedy hardness might undo him.

Only then did he sit back, looking down at this bounty before him. She was astonishing. Her taste was in his mouth, tart and sweet, and she sprawled out before him like a dream. He felt her beauty like a physical blow, as if Josselyn was shattering him simply by lying there.

And she was. He could feel it—everything inside of him turned to glass, then cracked into shards— as if he was defenseless.

As if he was hers.

It took him a mere moment to strip off his clothes and then he was coming down to her again, gathering her to him, so that at last they were naked together.

*At last.*

Cenzo knew that it had only been a month, but it felt to him like a lifetime. And even though he knew she was right, that he couldn't remember and lacked all context, he still had the bedrock certainty that he would feel the same no matter what he remembered.

Whatever his life might turn out to be, he needed her at its center.

It was nonnegotiable.

And he would prove it to her.

He positioned himself above her. Her eyes, dazed now, found his. His hardness moved through her slick heat, and he felt himself very nearly roar with the gut-punching pleasure of it.

"Cenzo," she managed to breathe out. "Cenzo, there's something I must tell you—"

"You can tell me anything you wish, *la mia amata*," he told her, his gaze locked to hers. His beloved. "Anything at all."

Josselyn blew out a breath. Her hands were pressed against his chest, but not, he thought, as if she wished to push him away so much as pull him close.

"I'm a virgin," she said.

He tried to take that in. He tried to make sense of it. But he couldn't. It was like a tidal wave, and there was nothing to do but swim.

"I told you, did I not?" Cenzo looked down at her as the wave hit him. Because there was only one truth. Only one conclusion. "You were always meant to be mine."

She shuddered, but he wasted no further time concerning himself with a foolish husband and a pointless marriage he did not pretend to understand.

Nor did he care. Not when there was this. *Her*.

He worked the hardest part of him into the mouth of her sex until he felt the resistance in all that slippery heat.

*Mine*, something roared inside him. *Always and forever mine.*

Then, heeding an instinct he could not have named, Cenzo drove himself inside her.

And as he did, something burst inside him, an interior explosion of light and echo, like an endless cascade.

It went on and on, even as below him, around him, Josselyn shattered anew.

Cenzo was lodged deep inside her. Her heat seemed to scald him as she cried out and the rocks bounced the sound of her pleasure back to him, like a symphony.

And he knew.

*He knew.*

After far too long stumbling about on the wrong side of that wall, Cenzo Falcone knew exactly who he was.

And what this wife of his had dared to do to him.

# CHAPTER TEN

IT FELT AS good as it hurt.

That was Josselyn's last and only thought before the power of it swept through her, leaving her
shaking, gasping, and little more than a mess of too
much sensation and need.

She had thought him big and strong as he'd stood
beside her on the altar. But his strength seemed new
to her now, braced above her on a soft blanket with
a curtain of bougainvillea behind them and the Sicilian blue all around.

New, too, because he was *in* her.

He was inside her, and the thought made her
clench down on that rampantly male part of him
so deep within her own body. Josselyn shuddered,
and she was pleased when she heard him hiss as if
he felt that same rush of pain melting into pleasure.

When she found his gaze again, he looked…dif-
ferent.

His predator's eyes were focused on her, intent in a different way.

A familiar way—

But then, before she could work out what that might mean, Cenzo began to move.

And all the things that had come before, each new sensation that had wrecked her and remade her, was like nothing compared to this.

The heat of him. That thick, impossible steel. The way he moved, each deep, drugging stroke teaching her that she knew nothing at all about her body, about the things she could feel, about what she'd been put on this earth to do.

For surely it was this. Two bodies become one, and in the becoming, this bliss. This joy, hot like fire and so sweet that it, too, hurt.

Josselyn wanted to hurt like this forever.

She wanted to keep her eyes on his, searching for something she couldn't have named if her life had depended on it. But instead, it was as if her eyelids were too heavy. They drifted shut, leaving her simply lost in the glory of this.

The rhythm of it. The advance and retreat.

As if they were no more and no less than the waves, the tide, the sea itself.

The sensation inside her sharpened, the glory of it expanded, and then everything broke apart—

And this time, as Josselyn spun out into nothing, she heard Cenzo let out a roaring sound, then fly away with her.

She had no idea how long it was they lay like that, his face buried in the crook of her neck, his weight too heavy and yet perfect. It was exactly what she most needed, just then. To be held and contained when she thought bits and pieces of her must have scattered from one end of the Mediterranean to the other.

And she felt as if she might cry when he finally stirred, pulling out of her body and shifting to one side. Though he pulled her with him, rolling her so she was braced there on his chest, and that was new. Different.

It was all so new and different, Josselyn could hardly make sense of it.

Her breasts felt huge and oversensitive and every time she breathed, they seemed to drag against his wonder of a chest to send new heat spiraling through her. His legs were strong and hair-roughened and the slide of her soft skin against them made her...quiver.

Josselyn suspected she was a mess, yet she couldn't seem to make herself care the way she usually would. Because she knew she shouldn't have let this happen, but she had to fight with herself to remember why. All she wanted was to do it again.

And again.

She wanted to go back in time and spend their whole month like this. Why had she spent these days playing such stupid games when she could have been learning all these mysteries that started and ended where his body and hers came together?

Cenzo smoothed her hair back. It took her a moment to really focus on him, this gorgeous man who knew her now as no other ever had. *Or ever would*, something in her whispered.

His gaze moved over her face and she could feel it like another touch. Her beauty mark, her lips. Each cheek, as if he was committing her to memory.

When she had long since done the same with him and those aquiline features, brutal and beautiful, that could have been stamped in steel, bronze or gold.

When his gaze met hers again, it seemed to punch through her, stealing her breath.

He lifted his head, and kissed her gently, sweetly, on her mouth.

Then regarded her steadily, that mouth of his unsmiling while his mythic eyes blazed.

"Cenzo?" she asked, something cold spinning inside her.

"Little wife," he replied, an edge to his voice she hadn't heard before. *Not in a month*, she corrected herself. And her face must have changed as the import of his words finally hit her—as that not quite endearment slapped at her—because he smiled. "Your tragedy, Josselyn, is that I remember everything."

Her heart stopped. Or maybe she only wished it did, because when it kicked into gear again, it made her whole body shudder.

She tried to push away from him, but for a long moment he held her fast—a quiet, unnecessary display of his superior strength.

Then he finally let her go, but the message was clear.

Josselyn hardly knew what to do with herself. She expected him to rage at her. Something dizzy inside her wheeled around and around and she wondered if he might simply toss her off the cliff, here where she doubted very much she would live through it the way he'd claimed she would before.

*You coward*, a voice inside her chimed in then, harshly. *It would be remarkably convenient if he did such a thing, wouldn't it? Then you would never need to face what you've done.*

Her hands were shaking as she struggled to pull her panties back on, then somehow fasten her bra with fingers like ice. She felt sheer relief when she finally pulled her dress back into place, and then stood, keeping her eyes on Cenzo.

Waiting for what must surely come next.

As she had always known it would, sooner or later.

He was standing now, dressing far more slowly than she had. Lazily, even. Josselyn wished that she could read his mind. That he would share his thoughts as he had this last month, but instead he only looked at the remains of their picnic there on the blanket.

"A servant," he said in wonderment, though there was that sharp, dark edge beneath it. "You made me a *servant*."

All of her justifications and rationalizations tasted like ash on her tongue, but she was a different woman now than the one who had married him, so filled with foolish hope. For one thing, she was no longer quite so naive. She had seen what she was capable of, how petty she could be, and there was no unknowing that.

But she was also terribly afraid that she had fallen in love with a man who did not exist.

A man she was married to, for good or ill.

"It is what you wanted to do to me," she reminded him, fighting to keep her voice level, and not quite succeeding. "Why is it so different?"

"My ancestors built this castle," he said, still in that same tone. "And you had me sleep on the stones they lay with their own bare hands. For a month."

"Wasn't that what was on offer to me?" Josselyn countered. "Either in a bed with you, the man who announced he wished to ruin me, or wherever I was most uncomfortable—isn't that what you said?"

He stared at her for a long moment, and it was as if she could see two men before her, one superimposed over the other. The ruthless man she had married, cruel and unconcerned with her feelings. And then the Cenzo who had lived with her here this past month, who had cared for her, worried over her, and made love to her.

One had made her a wife. The other had made her a woman.

And her heart felt firmly broken between the two.

He did not say another word, and that felt like a deeper indictment. Instead, he turned on his heel and started back up those stairs that had led them here.

Josselyn stayed behind, letting the adrenaline and all that leftover sensation wash through her, not surprised when she felt faintly sick. Rather than give into it, she busied herself with packing away their picnic and folding up the blanket. She did not look at the edge of the cliff again, for fear that strange near-joy that she'd felt at the rail far above one night would take her over again.

Because if it did she would never know if she wished to fly—or if she was taking the most expedient exit route away from this shamble of a marriage. And her own shameful part in it.

Cenzo had only threatened her, after all. She was the one who had actually gone through with it.

Eventually she started back up the stairs herself, one hand on the wall beside her. She concentrated only on the steps themselves, not the steep drop-off to one side, because looking at the water far below made her feel dizzy.

She made it back up to the gate, if slowly, and when she pushed her way through it, she braced herself for Cenzo. Would he be waiting? Would he be even more furious? Was it anxiety that charged through her...or anticipation?

But he wasn't there. She heard only her own footsteps echoing as she walked across the courtyard to let herself in the wooden door of this place she had been tempted to consider a kind of home of late. More fool her. It had only ever been a home of lies.

Inside, Josselyn walked carefully through the pretty rooms that flowed in and out of each other on the first level, her eyes moving this way and that to see if she could find him. For she had no doubt that she had not heard the last on the subject of her treachery.

But the more she thought about it, the more her own temper seemed to wake up inside her, blowing away the shame that had bloomed first.

Because he had planned to do these things to her. He'd been only too delighted to tell her all about it. She needed to remember that.

Not that two wrongs made a right, but it was important to remember that there *were* two wrongs. Not one. Not only hers.

She slid the picnic hamper onto the island in the kitchen, the blanket folded on top, and acknowledged that she'd expected to find him here. But the kitchen was ominously empty. Josselyn thought a moment, then set out to look for him. But it wasn't until she took the stairs down to an odd little gallery that ran along the side of the castle that she finally found him.

A place she had only ever visited once before, back when she'd arrived here.

Cenzo was standing, arms crossed and an unreadable expression on his beautiful face as he stared at a series of paintings on one wall. Across from him were three stained-glass windows, all sending a mad, giddy light dancing over him, tempting her to imagine that he was something other than dangerous.

When she knew better.

"Cenzo," she began.

But his hand moved, slashing through the air in a universal demand for silence, and the peremptory gesture made her jump slightly. And had its intended effect, because whatever words she thought she might say, they disappeared into the sudden constriction in her throat.

He did not look at her, keeping his gaze on the painting in front of him.

"Falcones do not divorce," he told her, his voice dark and low. "And that should not bring you comfort, little wife. It should terrify you unto your very bones. Because that means that I will never release you. I will never set you free. I will spend the rest of our lives making certain you understand exactly what it is that you did to me here. And paying for it. Again and again and again."

Her pulse picked up, but her temper came with it. "It's threats like those that lead a newly wedded wife to tell her husband, stricken though he is with sudden amnesia, that he's a servant. And threats like those that make it difficult to feel as badly about that as I should."

He turned to face her, his gaze a terrible fire. "Do not worry, Josselyn. I will make certain you feel as bad as you should. I will dedicate myself to the task."

She believed him. And she could see their life together, rolling out before her, dire and upsetting forever. It made her stomach knot.

"If I had it to do over again," she said, because it was true and she thought she owed him the truth, if nothing else, "I wouldn't tell you that you were my servant. Though I do not think it has done you any particular harm to spend a month imagining that, for once, you were something less than the center of the universe."

"I will thank you not to imagine you can decide whether or not I have been harmed."

"Cleaning a toilet does not actually harm a person, you know," she shot back at him. "Any suggestion it does is, at best, melodramatic."

He only lifted a cruel brow, and she missed the other version of him so much it stole her breath.

"Is that so, *cara*? Because you have spent so much time in your pampered life scrubbing toilet bowls?"

And she could see it then, the true force of his temper. She could see the blaze in his eyes easily enough. But more than that, she could see the way he held himself so still, so carefully, as if the slightest thread that held him together might snap at any moment—and he might, too.

Josselyn should have been terrified by that, but what she felt instead was something closer to exhilaration.

It didn't make sense. Then again, none of this made sense. She had been raised to be meek. To obey her father, because they both knew that no matter her feelings on the subject, he truly did have her best interests at heart. She'd gone along with this marriage because she'd trusted her father—and, she could admit now, because Cenzo was more work of art than man and she'd had foolish, girlish hopes.

But this past month had taught her that when push came to shove, she was not meek at all.

And maybe, in another scenario, that might have made her a monster.

Yet she rather thought that here, on this remote island where Cenzo had intended to enslave her with sex and isolation, it made her a contender.

At the very least it made her his equal.

"You can be as angry as you like," she told him, lifting her chin as if that could take the brunt of his glare. "But I think we both know that given the opportunity, you would have happily done the same."

His jaw was so tight that she could see a muscle flexing there. And his eyes were little more than a blaze.

"This is a portrait of my father," he told her, indicating the portrait beside him. "I looked at this portrait every day for a month and had no idea who I was looking at. I cannot forgive it."

"I understand." She meant to bite her tongue, but it was as if it had a mind of its own. "But I feel I should point out that you couldn't remember anything. You wouldn't have recognized him no matter what I told you."

Cenzo's gaze blazed hotter, and surely it should have scalded her. "He is the one who renovated this castle. Before his time, there was nothing to do here but camp out in ruins, think about our ancestors, and pray for deliverance. But he made it a home. He used to come here every summer and spend at least four weeks alone. He said he liked the conversation between himself, the sea, and the sky." He dragged in a breath. "One year he came back from his retreat, got into the car that waited for him, and instead of driving back to the Falcone villa Taormina, he drove himself halfway up Mount Etna. Then over the side of a cliff."

"I read about his accident," Josselyn said quietly. "I'm sorry."

And it was as if he erupted, though he still stood still.

She hardly knew how she remained standing.

"Don't you dare apologize to me," he growled at her. "Don't you dare, not with your wicked father's blood in your veins. Making you a monster like him."

That was a little too close to what she'd been thinking herself—and harder to dismiss when he said it. She focused on the part that wasn't her.

"Maybe now you can tell me what it is you think my father did to yours," Josselyn managed to get out. "When I can tell you that to his mind, your father was a friend. His best friend, who he misses to this day."

Cenzo looked as if he might explode, but he didn't. He took a moment to breathe instead, while every hair on the back of her neck stood up.

"My father made one phone call when he came back from the island that night," Cenzo said after a few moments had passed. "He called Archibald Christie, his old roommate and supposed friend. They spoke for ten minutes and then he drove off to kill himself. Your father has never divulged the content of that call, but my mother has a theory. She maintains that the phone call was the last step in a campaign of envy your father had been waging against mine for decades. And that night, he won."

"My father never envied yours," Josselyn said, her voice shaking from all the emotions she dared not show. Not here. "He considered him a brother."

"My mother tells a different tale," Cenzo shot back. "Of how your father always wanted her, and how he could not handle the fact that she did not want him in return. How he worked subtly to undermine his supposed best friend, always pretending he might support him and then instead disappearing. Sometimes for years and years. What kind of friend is that?"

"Which years?" Josselyn demanded. "Was it when my mother died? Along with my brother? My father became a widower as well as a single father overnight. What kind of friend was your father not to understand this?"

"He had a darkness in him," Cenzo told her, as if the words hurt him. As if he would have given anything not to say them. "It grew worse the older he got and your father preyed upon it. Instead of soothing my father's fears, he inflamed them. He pushed him, because he bitterly resented that the man you think he considered a brother had not suffered as he had. He made sure that he did."

"That's crazy," Josselyn breathed. "And entirely

false. If I were you, I would ask yourself why your mother would tell you such a story."

"Because it is true," Cenzo thundered at her, the stained-glass bathing him in color. "Your father was a poison to mine and he knew it. He took pleasure in it. I know he convinced you that his only aim in arranging a marriage between you and me was your safety, but that is not so. He wanted to make sure that he still had access to my mother and that he could still work his poison—this time, on me."

She wanted to laugh, but nothing was funny. And worse, she could see that Cenzo believed every word he said.

"Where is he, then?" Josselyn asked, her voice soft, but shaking. "I spoke to him when I last took the boat out. He did not demand to know where we were, so that he could race to my side and attempt to influence you. Nor did he attempt anything like that in the past two years—I know because I made his travel arrangements. He must be a terribly ineffectual villain."

"He plays a long game," Cenzo growled. "He is so good at it that you don't even know he's doing it."

"Cenzo, this is madness."

Josselyn tried to find even a hint of the man she knew in his stark features, but there was no hint of him. She had fallen in love with a man who didn't exist. When she'd known better. But she couldn't help wanting to somehow reach this version of Cenzo, too.

She tried again. "Whatever you may think of my father, however manipulative you might think he is, he loves his daughter. I am his only remaining child. If you believe nothing else about him, believe that."

"Yes, such love," Cenzo threw back at her. He prowled toward her, but she didn't back down. She didn't cringe away from him, or so much as step back an inch. Instead, she glared as if he didn't make her shake. Even when he wrapped his hands around her shoulders not hard, but with enough intention to make her quiver, down deep inside. "Such love indeed, that he would sell you to the highest bidder."

"It was an auction of one, as you are well aware."

"Such love, if you are to be believed, that he would deliver you to a man you hardly knew and wash his hands of you, that easily."

"I have already told you that his own arranged marriage turned into something beautiful. He thought he picked the best candidate for what he assumed would be a repeat."

He shook his head, his old coin gaze glittering. "You are delusional."

And she thought he meant that, too.

Josselyn didn't bother to argue the point. She doubted he would hear her. Instead, she held his gaze—and did not back down. "You are well and truly poisoned, Cenzo, but not by my father. He was happy enough to look you in the eye and shake your hand on the day he delivered his only daughter into your tender care. Yet your mother chose to hide. Why is that? If she is so certain that my father is the villain, why wouldn't she use the opportunity of her son's wedding to her enemy's daughter to set the record straight?"

"Because your family has done enough, damn you," Cenzo threw at her.

And then he was kissing her as if his life depended on it.

So she kissed him back in the same way, because she knew hers might. That was how wildly her heart thundered within her.

He swept her into his arms and carried her through the castle, up those winding stairs toward the top of the tower, and he did not spare so much as a glance for the landing where he had fallen a month ago.

Once in the sprawling master bedroom he threw her into the center of that wide bed where she had slept so many nights by herself, then followed her down.

This time they tore each other's clothes off. This time it was less a beautiful dance and more a different kind of combat. Wild and slick.

Hot and edgy.

"Do you think this will solve anything?" she demanded as he thrust inside her.

"It will solve one thing," he growled at her ear, as if his words were torn from him. "It will make this need less sharp."

But to Josselyn, every touch was sharper than knives.

And her curse was that she loved every cut.

Even if, when she woke the next morning, she was alone.

For a moment she was confused, especially because she could hear a sound she hadn't heard in some time—the motor of the large fishing boat that had brought her here.

She leaped from the bed and grabbed her wrapper as she ran, throwing it around her and somehow managing not to trip and kill herself on the stone stairs.

Josselyn raced down to the kitchen, where she had found Cenzo every morning since she'd come here, but it was empty again.

Save the note in bold, slashing handwriting on the island where her coffee and breakfast usually waited.

*Find your own way home, little wife. And take heed—I will come for you when it's time.*

She crumpled it in her hand, a terrible sob building inside her as she ran through the castle and out through the great wooden door. Then across the courtyard to the old gate.

When she pushed her way through and stood out on the wide steps, she could see the boat pulling away.

And the single, solitary figure standing out on the deck at the stern, his face tilted up toward the castle's heights as if he'd summoned her deliberately.

Just for the pleasure of leaving her behind.

# CHAPTER ELEVEN

THE FALCONE VILLA had stood in some or other form for centuries. Each generation made sweeping announcements about all the changes they would make to the historic structure, yet none ever managed to leave so much as a fingerprint.

That was the trouble with a bloodline like his, Cenzo knew. Nothing it touched was ever truly its own.

He remembered his childhood here, mostly spent in the company of nannies and other staff, because his father was always too busy managing the vast Falcone empire.

And his mother was always too busy.

Cenzo felt that same swell of bitterness in him as he found his way through the marble halls he knew so well. The same acrid rush that he'd been fighting since he'd left the Castello dei Sospiri.

It had been another long month.

And Cenzo had been avoiding this meeting.

First, he had indulged his rage. His fury. He had flown to his property in Paris and had availed himself of civilization. The finest restaurants, the most diverting shows. He had told himself he could not possibly miss his flirtation with servitude. He could not possibly find his bed too soft and his waking hours invaded by worries over the happiness of a woman who had betrayed him.

But Josselyn was all he thought about.

And it wasn't as if that faded as the weeks went by. It was only that the longing for her became so commonplace that other things found their way in, too. Like the things Josselyn had suggested about his mother.

Cenzo had dismissed them all, of course—but that didn't keep him from going over them again and again. Especially as he was neither the man who had married Josselyn, bent on revenge, nor the man who had served her. He was both of them, and neither, and nothing looked as it had.

Not his own reflection. Not the world he did not live in, but only inhabited, without her.

And not his mother, either.

He found Françoise where she always was at midday, lolling about in her dressing room and tending to her toilette. Because she did not rise before noon, no matter what. She insisted that her chocolate be placed at her bedside so she might sip it slowly as she considered the day before her. She had always been very particular. And so quick to share her opinions on all things that he had been certain she could not have a single one he hadn't heard.

In this past month, he hadn't been able to stop wondering what he'd missed.

Françoise saw him in the mirror of her vanity table and waved her staff away.

"I hope you've come to tell me of your success," she said when they'd gone. She sat in her favorite chair, there before her glass, critically examining her face. Ruthlessly looking for signs of age, he knew. He had once thought she was insecure, though he knew better now. "That you have reduced the girl to rubble and made it clear to her father exactly how you plan to treat her. Like the disposable whore she is."

Cenzo could remember, with perfect clarity, the man he'd been when he married Josselyn. He remembered all his plans in detail. He remembered the triumph he'd felt that she had fallen so easily into his clutches and how pleased he'd been that there was an attraction between them, because it would make his inevitable victory all the sweeter.

He could remember all of that, but the driving need to take revenge had deserted him. It had gotten tangled up in the way he'd served Josselyn for weeks, too deeply invested in her happiness to be able to swing that pendulum back to where it had been.

And savoring her innocence had not helped.

Because of those things, it was as if he saw the world in a different way. As if there were new colors and the old ones no longer made sense.

Not just the world in general, but *his* world. And his mother most of all.

"Your absence from the wedding was noted," he told her.

Cenzo would normally move farther into the room, but today he remained in the doorway.

"I should hope that my absence was noted." She let out an affronted little laugh. "I wanted to send a clear message."

And no matter how he had come at this problem, he always ended up in the same place. "I think you may have succeeded on that level, Maman. But I do not think it is the message you intended."

Françoise made a production of swiveling around in her chair so she could stare at him, her only son. Her only son and her only defender.

The sinking feeling inside him, his constant companion this last month, only got worse.

Because he had been heedless in his support of his mother, always. Heedless, reckless, desperate. She demanded no less.

And he, who had thought himself such an independent man, beholden to no one, had always, always done as she'd asked.

*You are well and truly poisoned, Cenzo, but not by my father*, Josselyn had said.

He hadn't believed that when she'd said it. But as time passed, it had seemed as if her words had grown barbed and weighted. And uncovered poison in him he never would have believed was there.

He still didn't want to believe it.

But he had spent a month of his life living without the driving need for revenge his mother had put in him. He remembered it too well.

That and the ghosts. The memories he'd never wanted to face.

Looking at her today, he felt empty.

"It is as I feared," his mother said, bristling. "You have fallen victim to the Christie girl. Yet another man felled by a taste of a common—"

"Careful, please," Cenzo said with a soft menace he did nothing to hide. "You are referring to my wife. The future mother of the heir to the Falcone legacy."

His mother gasped, but he could see her clearly now. He could see the calculation in her gaze—and he had to wonder if it had always been there. He feared it must have been. How had he missed it?

"I had every intention of crushing Josselyn beneath my heel," Cenzo told her, still trying to see what he must have seen before. Still trying to find some softness, some real emotion. But there was only her armored beauty and that narrow glare.

Cenzo could remember too many things now, and they were things he should have remembered before he hit his head. But it was as if having amnesia had only awakened him to all the ways in which he'd forgotten the most important parts of his own life. He'd been weaned on tales of the Falcone legacy as if it was the only thing that could possibly matter. And after his father had died, he had been reeling about in despair—and his mother had filled his head with enemies and blame.

It had seemed a natural progression. Grief was for lesser men, surely.

But now he remembered all the rest of it. The strain that had always hung between his parents. His father's increasing isolation and his mother's brittle refusal to curb her social engagements, no matter how many times the society pages printed those photographs of her with other men that made his father ill.

Françoise had spun that, too. *Your father can be jealous, but I persevere*, she would tell him as a boy, as if she was the hero of the tale. Or, *Your father is protective, that is all, for he alone knows the many wrongs that have been perpetrated against us both.*

Cenzo understood now that he had believed he had enemies long before he knew what that word meant.

But now he knew that his greatest enemy had always been the lies his mother told.

"I am not my father. I will not give you an infinite number of chances. I will ask you once. Did you proposition Archibald Christie?" And Cenzo smiled coldly while she sputtered. "And before you answer, you should know that he kept your letters."

Because he hadn't seen those letters, but he believed Josselyn.

*He believed her.*

Once he'd understood that, he'd come straight here. For he believed her, even now. Even after she had made him think he was a lowly servant.

Françoise held his gaze, but said nothing.

And as that silence drew out, Cenzo faced perhaps the most shameful truth yet.

That even now, even when he knew better, he had expected an explanation. Something to exonerate her.

"I applaud you for not lying," he managed to say. He let out a hollow laugh. "It shames me to admit I almost wish you would."

Josselyn had torn the scales from his eyes, and he couldn't close them again. He couldn't go back to his willful blindness.

He couldn't pretend.

"You told me he killed himself in despair," Cenzo said, every syllable that he uttered its own condemnation. "After a conversation with Archibald Christie."

"He spoke to Archibald after he left the island

and was dead soon after," Françoise replied haughtily. "What other conclusion can be drawn?"

"When did you last speak to him?" Cenzo asked softly. Because he'd spent hours and hours trying to get the facts to make sense with what Josselyn had showed him.

And her silence now confirmed his suspicions.

"He radioed you, didn't he?" he asked. "He couldn't call you from the island, but he often radioed in that year. You would lock yourself in his office and talk to him each night. And I always wondered why, when you told me he was depressed, it always sounded as if you were the one defending yourself. What was he accusing you of, Maman? I'm betting it was all those men you betrayed him with, over the years. And I bet that when he left the island, he called the man whose betrayal had hurt him the most, and first, only to discover the truth."

Her face only twisted. "You are wrong. He was a sad, ill man."

"He was a good man," Cenzo said, his voice thicker than he would have liked. "And he was a Falcone. He never would have killed himself. He drove halfway up Mount Etna so he would not come here in a temper, didn't he? You should never have let me believe otherwise."

And he faced the fact that even then, there was a part of him that wanted her to deny it. To explain all the little things he'd taken much too long to put together. To shine a different light on events that made them all make sense—and allowed him to revere her as he always had.

But she didn't.

Because there was no getting past the letters, was there? She'd written letters, Josselyn had read them, and he would rather have acted the servant for years than have to face what that meant.

"Cenzo," his mother said then, reaching out to him—no doubt reading the resolve on his face. "Cenzo, my son, this girl has confused you."

"On the contrary." He straightened from the doorway. And when he looked at his mother, he finally saw her. He finally, fully, saw her for who she was. Sheer poison, as Josselyn had known when he had not. He supposed that was one more thing he would have to live with. "Remember, please, that everything you consider yours is mine. Do not try to play your games with my wife. Or her father. You may stay here in this villa and rot—but if you test me, Maman, I promise you I will throw you out on the street. With my own hands."

She gaped at him. "You would not dare."

"I would advise you not to try me," Cenzo bit out.

That was how he left her, sputtering still. He had no intention of returning.

And now the weight of her lies was gone, only one thing remained.

The most important thing.

# CHAPTER TWELVE

CENZO PRESENTED HIMSELF at the Christie estate in Pennsylvania the next morning. He had expected the door to be opened by staff, but instead it was Archibald himself who peered out into the November early morning gloom.

And did not smile.

"It appears you have already made my daughter unhappy," the older man said, though he still stepped back and beckoned Cenzo within.

"I intend to make it up to Josselyn," Cenzo said stiffly, "but I must also apologize—"

Archibald stopped him, there in the grand foyer where Cenzo had given Josselyn the Sicilian Sky long ago. "You forget that I chose you for my daughter. And I'm well aware that you thought me a fool. But I'm not one. You remind me of your father."

Cenzo's chest was too tight. His throat felt thick. What would have happened if he'd allowed this man to speak with him the way he'd wished to do before the wedding? Instead of steering the conversation away from his father every time? "Thank you."

"I have never known a finer man," Archibald said. His dark eyes gleamed with compassion, and something else. "It's not only Josselyn that I wish to see happy in this marriage, son. I know that your father would expect me to do this. To make sure, as he could not, that you find the peace he never could."

Two months ago, Cenzo would not have recognized the sensation that washed through him, then. But he knew it now.

"You humble me," he managed to say. And then, "I will not let you down again."

And old Archibald Christie smiled, cannily. "See that you don't, son. See that you don't."

He led Cenzo through the house, in and out of rooms gleaming with the kind of quiet elegance he associated with his wife. Then out into the back, where a covered walkway led to a fogged-up greenhouse.

Archibald inclined his head, then left Cenzo to it.

He pushed his way inside, the humidity enveloping him instantly. There was music playing, a female singer crooning something heartbreakingly wry. He moved between the rows of plants, then stopped dead when he saw her.

His Josselyn. At last.

She had piled her hair up on the top of her head and was wearing a kind of smock over her usual uniform. Jeans and a T-shirt, both simple and sophisticated at once. Like her.

The very sight of her walloped him. She hadn't even turned around to note his presence, and still, he felt as if she'd sucker punched him.

And again, his memories did him no favors. Because all he could remember now was her. Not his plans before he hit his head. Not his certainty in himself after. All of that and then none of it, because all there was in the center, holding up the world, was Josselyn.

She glanced over her shoulder, then froze, taking her time to turn around and meet his gaze.

He didn't know what he'd expected. But it wasn't the grave way she regarded him now.

"You told me you would come. In your note."

He had forgotten he'd written a note. "I did."

"I thought it would be a while. Years, perhaps." She studied him. "I assumed public humiliations would play a part."

He thought of the way she'd sobbed in his arms as she'd taken her pleasure, again and again. The look on her face when he had told her he lost his memory. Cenzo had spent this whole month since he'd last seen her replaying every single thing that had ever happened between them. Over and over again.

And he did not want her gravity.

"You told me you wanted this marriage to work,

Josselyn." He lifted a brow. "That you thought we were lucky because we did not start off muddled by romantic notions."

She looked away for a moment, and when she looked back at him she looked more sad than grave. It was not an improvement.

"You don't have to mock me," she said with quiet dignity. "If there was something I could do to take back what happened, I would do it. But I can't."

His jaw felt like granite. "Which part of what happened?"

Josselyn took a visible breath, as if gathering herself. "Making you my servant. It was petty. I regretted it almost immediately, but I couldn't take it back. I apologize."

Cenzo hadn't anticipated an apology. Not *to* him.

"You regretted it, yet you had me cleaning windows and scrubbing floors," he said dryly. "It seems to me that you owe me."

And then he had to bite back a smile. Because he had become adept at reading each and every one of her expressions while serving her. He knew that flush on her cheeks. He knew that particular shine in her eyes.

He was Cenzo Falcone, as close to a king as a man could be without a crown. And once a humble manservant.

In both lives, he had always gotten what he wanted.

He did not intend for that to change now that he was both men. Now that he had learned both lessons.

"Cenzo," Josselyn said then, sounding…breathless. "Can we just…start over?"

And he moved closer to her, so he was directly in front of her. Close enough that he could have swept her into his arms. He could have kissed her silly, as every part of him longed to do.

But instead, he held her gaze.

And then, heeding the urge of the man he hoped he would become, not the versions he'd been, he dropped to one knee before her.

"I don't want to start over," he told her, every truth he'd discovered along the way in his voice. His gaze. "I don't want to forget a single moment, Josselyn. I want to remember them all. From the moment you came into that room in a cottage in Maine and upended everything. I took you to a ruined castle and thought that I would turn you into rubble, but you are the one who leveled me."

Her beautiful eyes widened. "Cenzo…" she whispered.

But he kept on. "How can I condemn you for the trick you played on me when what I planned to do to you was worse? Some would call it karma. But I call it a miracle." He reached over and took her hands in his, that stone that had cursed so many before him reminding him of what mattered. The sea and the sky and the place they were one. And this woman, who made all of them shine. "Because whether I remembered myself or not, there was you. And I am not too proud to use the debt you feel to keep you with me. To prove to you that despite everything I have done to you, and wanted to do to you, you are the one who won after all."

She looked fierce, even as that shine in her eyes spilled over into tears. "I don't want to win. I don't want either one of us to win, because that means someone has to lose. And what kind of life is that?"

"Josselyn—" he began.

But she silenced him by tugging her hands free and pressing her palms to his cheeks. Bringing her face to his as he still knelt there before her.

"I lost my mother and my brother in an instant. An afternoon storm and that was it. They were gone." Her voice was urgent and low. Her gaze was intense. "Life is so fleeting, Cenzo, and it can end so quickly. You could have died in that fall. And if all you think about is winning and losing, taking revenge and plotting against your enemies, don't you see? You're going to miss the whole thing."

He did see. He saw her, and nothing else had made sense since. Not until he'd found his way back to her.

"I have been two men for you," he told her then. "And I have spent this last month desperately trying to pretend that at least one of them was a lie, but

I keep coming back to a single, inescapable truth. I wanted to bind you to me. I wanted to make you unfit for anything at all but my bed. And instead it is I who might as well be rubble beneath your shoe, Josselyn. You humbled me, and yet I think you saved me. Because had you not, I would never know." He lifted a hand and held hers, there where it still lay against his cheek. "Had you not toppled me from the height of my arrogance, I could never have known how much I loved you. How much I will always love you. And whether this life is long or short, none of it will matter at all unless I keep on loving you. Forever."

She whispered his name as if it was a prayer. "Do you know, all the while I was making you clean and cook and serve me, all I really wanted was you. Not the you I'd already met and married, but the one you showed me every night. Not twisted, but real. Fascinating and beautiful, commanding and breathtaking, and that was when you thought you were a humble man with a humble life. I wanted you then." Josselyn blew out a shaky breath. "And if I'm honest, I wanted you before. My father wanted me to marry a man of his choosing, it's true. But if it hadn't been you, there's no way I would have gone through with it. It was always you, Cenzo. Whatever version of you. It was still you."

"I love you," Cenzo told her, gazing up at her. "I

want you to marry me, again. Just you and me, the sky and the sea, and who knows what we can do?"

"I will," she whispered. "I will marry you, again. I love you too. Because I have seen both sides of you, dark and light. Cruel and caring. And I have loved them both."

"I cannot promise that I won't revert to form." He took the hand that wore his ring and pressed his fingers to the blue stone that proclaimed her a Falcone. And forever his. "I can only promise that going forward, it will not take a knock on the head to put me right again. All it will take is you, my beautiful wife. My only love. Believe in me and I promise, I will be the man you deserve."

"And I will be the wife that you need," she promised him. "No pettiness or poison, Cenzo. Only this. Only us."

Tears still slid down her cheeks as she bent to him and kissed him at last. First a sweet seal on these vows they'd made today, but then the roar of his dragon rose up, becoming part of that fire that burned between them.

Passion, not poison.

Bright, hot, and theirs, forever.

And then she was in his arms, or perhaps he was in hers, and everything was that heat, that need, that impossible, glorious greed—and all of that was love. Every touch, every whisper, every sigh.

All of it was love, and he knew, then, that it would be like that forever.

They rolled this way and that, there in all that humidity, the air thick and perfumed with growing things.

It felt like a new beginning. It felt like spring, here in a dark November.

Because Josselyn's eyes were bright and her smile was beautiful, and she looked at him as if all she saw was the man he vowed, there and then, he would always be for her.

Always.

She settled herself astride him, still smiling as she looked down at him. His hands found her waist, and they both sighed a little, fully clothed as they still were, as the hardest part of him found that soft sweetness that was only his. Only and ever his.

"I love you," he told her, in every language he knew.

But her eyes lit up in the same way they had when she'd told him he was a servant.

"I promise you this, husband," Josselyn said, mischief in her voice and forever in her eyes. "You will never know a moment's peace. Your life with me will be a delicious agony. I will make you an addict for my touch, my gaze, the barest possibility of my approval."

His own words said back to him were electrifying. They made his heart pound. They made him hunger to taste her again. He wondered if they'd had the same effect on her, back then.

Josselyn leaned closer. "You will live for it. For me."

"This does not sound like a threat, my little wife."

She placed her fingers over his mouth and he nipped at them, making her laugh. "And I will do the same. We will be riotously happy. We will make each other feel safe, you and I. We will not be junkies, Cenzo, because we will know joy. We will raise our children swathed in it. And we will live, as long as we can, loving each other more. And more. And always still more."

"More," he agreed.

Because he was Cenzo Falcone. He would see to it.

And then he started as he meant to go on, there on the floor of her father's greenhouse, making both of them laugh, then groan.

Until, at last, they made each other whole.

And kept right on doing it for the rest of their lives.

\* \* \* \* \*

*If you loved* The Sicilian's Forgotten Wife
*you're sure to love these other stories*
*by Caitlin Crews!*

Christmas in the King's Bed
His Scandalous Christmas Princess
Chosen for His Desert Throne
The Secret That Can't Be Hidden
Her Deal with the Greek Devil

*Available now!*

## #3945 HER BEST KEPT ROYAL SECRET
*Heirs for Royal Brothers*
by Lynne Graham

Independent Gaby thought nothing could be more life-changing than waking up in the bed of the playboy prince who was so dangerous to her heart... Until she's standing in front of Angel a year later, sharing her shocking secret—his son!

## #3946 CROWNED FOR HIS DESERT TWINS
by Clare Connelly

To become king, Sheikh Khalil must marry...immediately. But first, a mind-blowing whirlwind night with India McCarthy that neither can resist! When India reveals she's pregnant, can a ring secure his crown...and his heirs?

## #3947 FORBIDDEN TO HER SPANISH BOSS
*The Acostas!*
by Susan Stephens

Rose Kelly can't afford any distractions. Especially her devilishly attractive boss, Raffa Acosta! But a week of networking on his superyacht may take them from professional to dangerously passionate territory...

## #3948 SHY INNOCENT IN THE SPOTLIGHT
*The Scandalous Campbell Sisters*
by Melanie Milburne

Elspeth's sheltered existence means she's hesitant to swap places with her exuberant twin for a glamorous wedding. But the social spotlight is nothing compared to the laser focus of cynical billionaire Mack's undivided attention...

---

**YOU CAN FIND MORE INFORMATION ON UPCOMING HARLEQUIN TITLES, FREE EXCERPTS AND MORE AT HARLEQUIN.COM.**

HPCNMRB0921

*Kitty will do anything for the foundation inspired by her
tumultuous childhood. Even agree to a fake relationship
to help Laurence, the impossibly guarded man from
her past, land his next deal. Only, their chemistry is
anything but make-believe!*

*Read on for a sneak preview of debut author
Jadesola James's new story for Harlequin Presents,*
Redeemed by His New York Cinderella.

"I'll speak plainly." The way he should have in the beginning,
before she had him ruminating.

"All right."

"I'm close to signing the man you met. Giles Mueller. He's the
owner of the Mueller Racetrack."

She nodded.

"You know it?"

"It's out on Long Island. I attended an event close to it once."

He grunted. "The woman you filled in for on Friday is—was—
my set date for several events over the next month. Since Giles
already thinks you're her, I'd like you to step in. In exchange, I'll
make a handsome donation to your charity—"

"Foundation."

"Whatever you like."

There was silence between them for a moment, and Katherine
looked at him again. It made him uncomfortable at once. He knew
she couldn't see into his mind, but there was something very
perceptive about that look. She said nothing, and he continued
talking to cover the silence.

"You see, Katherine, I owe you a debt." Laurence's voice was
dry. "You saved my life, and in turn I'll save your business."